Ans			
ASH			(Lv2)
Bev			
C.C.			
C.P.		Ott	
Dick		PC	
DRZ		PH	
ECH		P.P.	
ECS		Pion.P.	
Gar	03/05	Q.A.	7/05
GRM		Riv	
GSP		RPP	
G.V.		Ross	
Har		S.C.	
JPCP		St.A.	
KEN		St.J	
K.L.		St.Joa	
K.M.		St.M.	
L.H.	03/06	Sgt	
LO		T.H.	01/09
Lyn		TLLO	
L.V.	8/27	T.M.	2/05
McC		T.T.	
McG		Ven	
McQ		Vets	
		VP	
		Wed	
		W.L.	

FIT TO KILL

It took a little while for Blake Denton to realize that the redhead was playing a game with him. But when this did become clear, he decided to go along with her for the ride. It was an ill-considered decision, as time was to prove. Apart from the kicks involved and the monetary reward, there were other, sinister factors lurking in the background of which Denton knew nothing. When he did finally grasp the full horror of his position it seemed much too late to withdraw.

MARK KANE

FIT TO KILL

Complete and Unabridged

LINFORD
Leicester

First published in Great Britain in 1972 by
Robert Hale Limited
London

First Linford Edition
published 2004
by arrangement with
Robert Hale Limited
London

British Library CIP Data

Kane, Mark
    Fit to kill.—Large print ed.—
Linford mystery library
1. Detective and mystery stories
2. Large type books
I. Title
823.9'14 [F]

ISBN 1–84395–537–7

Published by
F. A. Thorpe (Publishing)
Anstey, Leicestershire

Set by Words & Graphics Ltd.
Anstey, Leicestershire
Printed and bound in Great Britain by
T. J. International Ltd., Padstow, Cornwall

This book is printed on acid-free paper

1

Claire Paige had rarely spoken more than two consecutive words to Blake Denton during the three months he had been working for *Advance Mail Order* until the morning Denton picked up the five-dollar bill from the office floor and stuffed it into his hip pocket.

Then she said coldly and contemptuously, 'Put that back where you found it.'

She had swivelled on her chair to glare at Denton, although, a moment ago — before stooping to palm the bill surreptitiously — he had been certain no one was paying the slightest attention to him.

His skin burned as he looked at the redhead. He was a brawny six-footer, heavy and strong in the shoulders but slim in the waist and hips. He had a craggy jaw and a broad forehead, and his dark hair was crew-cut into a prickly cap that gave him the appearance of a boxer or wrestler.

The redhead was in her early twenties. She had good features and lush curves. What she had, too, was a refrigerated manner that had begun to rankle on Denton after his first few days working near her. She might as well have carried a 'Hands Off' sign around with her for the way she treated Denton and everyone else who worked in the dispatch office of the warehouse. Everyone except Hank Otis, that was.

Hank and Jack Rhodes were partners in the firm, and if rumour had it right the pair of them had commenced their lucrative mail order outfit in the attic of a skidrow apartment house twenty years before. Rhodes took care of advertising and marketing while old Hank looked after the dispatch side of the business.

Clare Paige — or Miss Paige, as she was to be addressed — was Hank's private secretary. She was in charge of his letters and phone calls and arranged all his business appointments. She occupied the desk over by the large window overlooking Cable Street, and it might have been a throne she sat on for the stiffly regal attitude she adopted towards the lesser toilers in the office.

There was no doubt that Claire Paige was extremely efficient. She handled her work with a coolness and unruffled speed that gave the impression of everything else in her orbit having frozen still.

Old Hank would come and bend over her while he talked in his scratchy voice. He was sixty-two and affected a sober black suit and white, high-collared shirt with bowtie. While he talked his right hand would invariably stray tentatively to the girl's shoulder, and then, as the conversation progressed, the hand would slide on down to Claire Paige's waist. Denton had been watching the byplay since his arrival with cynical amusement, and wondered how long it would take the old guy to dip his hand finally to the magnet of those hips that shot out in swollen provocation over the edge of her chair.

Had Denton been in Hank Otis' shoes he would have reached her hips during the first week of her employment and at this stage he would be taking Claire on weekend tours of the best hotels. But Hank seemed to be stuck at a road-block.

Hank wasn't in the office just then. He had gone off somewhere a half-hour ago, leaving Claire to keep tabs on Denton, Sally Baines and Kirk Mason, the other two clerks, and the youth Jimmy Florian, who shuttled between the offices in the building and warehouse proper on the ground floor.

Sally Baines and Kirk Mason were slogging away at their typewriters in the far end of the big room and Jimmy was carrying a message to Jack Rhodes, so that no one appeared to have noticed Denton pick up the bill nor Claire Paige swing about to challenge him for approaching it.

'I might have dropped it,' he said tautly, his grey eyes meeting the green hazel-flecked ones which pinned him down with all the weight and coldness of a block of ice.

'You didn't, you know, Denton,' she said in a flat tone designed to reach nobody's ears but his own. 'I've seen it there since Mr Otis left. I thought it was a scrap of paper. It must have fallen from Mr Otis' wallet.'

Denton gave her a sly grin.

'Who are you kidding, Claire? Anything goes into Hank's wallet is a long-term prisoner.'

The girl showed her white teeth in a blatant sneer.

'That is no way to talk of Mr Otis, Denton, and you know it. And I'll thank you to call me Miss Paige. Now,' she went on more thinly, 'are you going to hand over the money, or would you rather take it up with Mr Otis? I don't have to spell out what he'll do to settle the matter.'

Denton could have spat in her eye. But no, he decided, he wouldn't want to do anything so unrewarding. He wanted to grab her and shake the hell out of her, rattle the starch from her spine, grab her by the pants, maybe and listen to her give a blood-curdling scream. That would cause joy all round.

For a brief spell they eyed each other in silent challenge and defiance. Finally, Denton brought the five-dollar bill from his hip pocket and dropped it on the floor where he'd found it.

He heard the girl's sharp intake of breath, saw her fury building.

'Give it to me,' she demanded quietly.

'You told me to leave it where I found it.'

'Do you want to start something?' she panted in an angry whisper. 'Bring the money over here.'

He lifted the bill and went over to her. He placed it on her desk although she was extending her fingers to take it. Her cheeks coloured darkly and her eyes took little savage bites out of him. Her bosom strained heavily against her blouse.

'Thank you, Denton. You'd better return to your desk and get busy with those invoices. Mr Otis wants me to mail them on my way to lunch.'

'Sure,' Denton said curtly. 'Sure, Miss Paige.'

He regarded her steadily and searchingly for a moment, then wheeled over the room to reach his typewriter and the pile of invoices he had to attend to.

Seated, he glanced across his shoulder and saw Claire Paige put the five-dollar bill away in her handbag. She kept a small mirror perched on the window in front of her, ostensibly to see herself fluff her hair and touch up her lips with rouge before leaving at lunchtime and in the afternoon, but the mirror was so positioned that she could peer into it and see Denton's head and shoulders where he sat at his typewriter. She was staring at the mirror just then and their eyes met. She lowered her head and went on with her work.

Denton chewed his underlip thoughtfully, wondering what the blazes was going on. For three months the dame had treated him as though he hardly existed, and then, suddenly, she had set that scene so she could have a clash with him. He was sure it had been a deliberate set-up. But why?

He could guess why. She hated him so much she wanted rid of him. When Otis got back she would run over at the mouth about the five-spot and advise old Hank he was a thief whom they would be better rid of.

He knew why she hated him. He didn't conform in the way that Sally and Kirk and the youth Jimmy conformed. They were round pegs in round holes; he was the exception. He didn't fit into any shape of hole — pigeonhole or any other variety. Therefore he baffled her, unnerved her, perhaps. And if the truth were told she might be frightened of him.

There was a laugh. What had he done or said to frighten her? He had come to *Advance* via an employment agency. He had been planning on an art career when call-up and Vietnam came along to disrupt his plans. He had been flown home with a busted leg. The leg — his left one — had taken a packet of shrapnel, but the surgeons in the military hospital had performed a minor miracle on the limb. True, he had been left with a bad limp for almost a year, but these days the limp was scarcely perceptible, and the slight stiffness that plagued him now and then was nothing to worry him seriously.

He could be a dead man at this moment and he knew it. It made him grateful in an odd, bitter fashion, having seen so many of his comrades cut down, as though a senseless scythe had run amuck in a bed of blossoming flowers.

After his experiences the idea of a career in art had seemed silly; any kind of career had seemed silly. As both his parents were dead he was a free agent and he preferred the insecurity of drifting from one job to another to finding a niche that he might widen into his own private foxhole. But lately he had taken an interest in automobiles, and the notion had come to him that he might get a small garage going if he could save enough money to take the scheme off the ground.

He was an accomplished typist and shorthand writer, and the employment agency he had gone to here in Maxwell had channelled him to the mail order company. The work was tedious at times, but the salary was reasonable, and he planned to carry on with the firm for a few more months at least.

★ ★ ★

He tensed when old Hank returned to the office twenty minutes later. He had bought a carnation for his lapel and gravitated to Claire Paige's desk, smiling and sliding on to the chair she pulled out for him.

He began a lengthy talk and the girl made notes. She would wait until the boss man was through before giving him the lowdown on the incident of the five-spot.

He was amazed when Hank Otis left Claire Paige presently and went towards his own cubby-hole at the rear. Hank glanced at Denton on his way past.

'How are things this morning, Blake?'

'Coming along nicely, Mr Otis, thanks.'

'Good, Blake, good!'

He went on to the door of his office, but hesitated and then came back to Denton. Denton was typing out a blue invoice and paused to look up.

'Something you want to say to me, Mr Otis?'

Hank Otis was pale-featured and boney, with flat, bloodless lips and blue, washed out eyes. He always reminded Denton of someone who had lately risen from a sickbed, and yet there was a drive and energy lurking behind the weakly façade which was quite astonishing. He had taken a shave whilst he was out, and the distinctive after-lotion used by his barber had the tang of sagebrush.

'Yes, there is, Blake. You've been with us for what — three, four months, I guess?'

'Three months, Mr Otis. Three full months and four days.' Otis smiled faintly, his washed-out eyes brightening. 'You like it here okay, Blake?'

This was it now, Denton told himself. Claire Paige had blown the gaff on him, but had added a rider for mercy. His nerves bunched.

'Yes, I do like it,' he acknowledged steadily. 'I can cope with the work. I'm never made to keep at it until I sweat. All in all, I'm quite happy here.'

'Good, good, Blake! That's fine, that's swell.'

He was leaving and Denton spoke at his back.

'Oh, Mr Otis . . . '

Hank stopped and spun round, mild annoyance pulling at the flat lips. He hated being robbed of the initiative.

'What is it?'

'You dropped a five-spot — I mean a five-dollar bill before you left earlier. I picked it off the floor and gave it to Miss Paige.'

'Oh! But I don't think it was my money, Blake. Thanks anyhow.'

'A pleasure, Mr Otis.'

The girl had been watching them in her scrap of mirror and Denton saw her shoulders stiffen as Hank Otis retraced his steps to her desk. They talked for several minutes and then Claire Paige reached for her handbag. Old Hank made a motion for her to put it aside without opening it and at last she did so. There was a deeper colour in her cheeks now than Denton had ever seen. Hank Otis left her and headed straight to his office. When the door banged on him Denton's gaze sought the girl. Her shoulders remained stiff but she didn't look in the mirror. Her fingers were flicking over the keyboard of her electric typewriter like the probing fangs of miniature snakes.

*   *   *

Kirk Mason had noticed more than Denton imagined. He and Kirk used the same diner on Pollard Street at lunchtime, and when they were seated at their table he asked what the fuss with the Snow Queen had been in aid of.

Mason was a lean, sallow-featured, dyspeptic man of forty, who didn't get enough fresh air and who smoked too many cigarettes. He was married to an ailing woman who continually nagged him, so that he had a harried, nervous air about him. He liked Denton a lot, seeing everything in the big, rugged character that he never was and wished he had been.

Once he had invited Denton home to his small southside bungalow for supper, and Denton had accepted. The single experience of the saw-tongued ailing wife had been enough for Denton, and although other invitations had been forthcoming he had politely refused them.

Still, he and Kirk always had lunch together, and sometimes, after the day's work was over, they would have a few beers together in Wally's Bar at the end of Cable Street before Denton went home to his bachelor apartment out on Ethna Road.

'Nothing much,' Denton grunted in answer to Mason's question. He saw no reason to withhold what had actually happened, and at the end of his recital Mason pursed his thin lips thoughtfully.

'That isn't like the Snow Queen, Blake. Trying to put you on the spot, I mean. She might be the original frigid Brigid, but beneath that marble exterior there beats a heart of pure gold.'

Kirk went on to describe how she had negotiated a rise in salary for him without his knowledge after he had been six months with *Advance*.

'That was before Sally was shifted to our department and when there was plenty of work landing on my desk. I laboured like a galley slave because I needed the job badly and I wanted to prove myself.' Kirk Mason smiled ruefully. 'So there was Claire — excuse me! Miss Paige — telling old Hank how I was worth more than he was paying me. Hank brought me into his sanctum and explained. Miss Paige reckoned I was due an extra twenty bucks a month and he had given the matter his full consideration. The upshot was I got the rise. I thanked the Snow Queen, but she seemed put out at Hank divulging her good deed. It was okay, she told me, and she'd rather not hear anything more about it. But, Blake, if the money belonged to Hank why didn't she give it to him?'

'He wouldn't take it,' Denton said shortly. 'It must have been her own money. If I'd thought that, I wouldn't have touched it.'

'Maybe it was bait to get on terms with you, Blake.' Mason laughed. 'Well, you never know. There comes a time when even the most virtuous virgin sees virginity as a stumbling block to the fuller and happier life.'

Denton grinned crookedly.

'Not for me, Kirk pal. Fire is fire and ice is ice and never the twain shall meet.'

'Cute but corny, old son. Fire has been known to melt ice. If you want my humble opinion, she is interested in you but wanted to test your honesty before committing herself. Dames do have a thing on honesty, believe it or not.'

'Then I goofed. Hurrah.'

'Maybe. I might have goofed myself. Money on the ground is rare, but fair game in the very best circles. And finders, keepers is mighty strong medicine. Here . . . have a cigarette and forget it, Blake. The Snow Queen moves in mysterious ways . . . '

★ ★ ★

Denton put the matter out of his head until five o'clock came round and it was time to close shop for the day. Sally and Kirk called so-long and left the office together. Next, Hank Otis emerged from his office, glanced at Denton and paused as if deliberating. He nodded abstractedly and went on to Claire Paige's desk. They spoke for a few minutes and Hank left. The girl was covering her typewriter and peered over at him.

'Time to lock up, Denton,' she said in a dry, impersonal tone.

'Coming. Just clearing my desk.'

She was standing patiently by the door when he joined her. She wore a green checked suit jacket which matched her skirt and looked like a million dollars. A boldness lifted in Denton. When he smiled at her, twin faint spots of colour touched her cheeks and she dropped her eyes briefly.

'Thanks for covering for me,' he said.

'Where did you get that idea?' Her red lips firmed over her white teeth. 'I didn't cover for you. I don't make a habit of covering for anyone.'

'No kidding?' He hesitated although she had the door partly open in a hint for him to get through it. 'So it was your own five-spot?'

'Never mind, Denton. Come along now.'

'You wanted to test me out, huh? I fell by the wayside. At the very first hurdle.'

'Please . . . Are you going?'

'Sure. But you know what, Claire baby, I'm going to ask you to have dinner with me. Don't bother telling me where you live. I know already. I'll call for you at

17

six-thirty. 'Bye until then.'

He left her staring after him, the white teeth gnawing at the red underlip, the green, hazel-flecked eyes glowing strangely.

2

At six-twenty Denton drove his three-year-old Volkswagen into St Ann's Avenue to reach the Biltmore apartment block.

Claire Paige lived well beyond the city's business line, in a modern zone that would look from the air as though it had been rather badly stitched on to the eastern suburbs of Maxwell. The impression would have been given by the curving road that was being laid across the area where the old and new joined. Part of the road was as yet nothing more than a violent gash in the earth and rock sub-strata, and the traffic jouncing over the rubble and clay set up a perpetual pall of dust.

Denton parked at length on the newly-laid asphalt frontage of the apartment block and entered the vestibule to ride the elevator to the seventh floor and number 714. He was wearing his best dark-blue lightweight suit and a snappy felt hat, and he whistled softly in his teeth as he pressed the bell button and heard a dim melodious chime inside.

He had been making bets with himself all of the way from Ethna Road to St Ann's Avenue. At the outset he had been laying himself odds of ten to one against Claire Paige paying any heed to his invitation, but by the time he parked on the forecourt he was thinking in terms of twenties; now, however, his optimism had suddenly sprung to the fore and the starting price had shortened dramatically to even money. It was as if his earlier hunch concerning the girl's motives had gained strength and weight. He would soon see, he decided.

He rang twice before the door opened and Claire Paige stood there. She was wearing a crisp linen dress with a light wrap over her shoulders, and her reddish hair was brushed until it sparkled with highlights. She was a sight to take any man's breath away. She smiled faintly, glancing at the small gold watch on her wrist.

'Six-thirty on the dot. You're very

punctual, Denton.'

'That's me,' he said with a wide grin. 'Always punctual when I'm calling on a beautiful dame. But try saying Blake a few times, won't you?'

'If you don't refer to me as a dame.'

She had shed most of her customary stiffness, which was truly remarkable, Denton thought. She was showing the real person under the stiffness, and he much preferred the relaxed Claire Paige to the very formal and horribly efficient Miss Paige.

'Shall we go,' he suggested cheerfully. 'And might I say you look wonderful?'

'You may.' She locked the door of her apartment with her latchkey and let him hold her arm on the way to the elevator. A subtle scent radiated from her person and she strode out lithely in step with him.

It was all too easy, Denton reflected as they reached the waning sunlight and he saw her seated in his car. He wondered if, basically, and unknown to the employees at *Advance*, she was an easy mark for the guy bold enough to brave the icicles that

21

were nothing but a front, or if, on the other hand, she had some sound reason for relenting to his particular charm.

He would find this out soon enough, also.

He took her to a midtown restaurant where they had a substantial but relatively inexpensive meal, and from there he took her to a nightclub in the fun belt. So far they talked only in generalitites, but Denton had the feeling there was something more significent in the wind.

There was a good floor-show at the nightclub and Claire appeared to be genuinely enjoying herself. She was a careful drinker, Denton noted, and not the sort you would prime with a load before swinging her back to your pad. Her eyes flashed when she looked at him and the mouth was warm with a sensual quality that stirred him powerfully. The linen dress was low-cut and set off her breasts to the best advantage, and when she found Denton staring, her eyes held his steadily for several seconds.

Denton was drinking more than he ought to.

'You ought to slow down, Sir Galahad. The cops in this town show little mercy to drivers with bug-eyes.'

'But you can drive me home, honey.'

'It's no excuse for making a pig of yourself, Blake.'

There was a sharpness to her tone which bit into Denton and had him wondering again. He had reached the stage where he saw the situation in innocuous terms. There was nothing sinister or ominous to be read into the girl's acceptance of his invitation. But her sharp tone brought him up short; it implied how he might easily disappoint her. Once again he was on the alert for the concealed motive. He took the hint and spaced out his drinks. When his hand closed over her fingers she made no attempt to drag them away.

'I kind of like you after all, Snow Queen.'

'Snow Queen?' She laughed. 'Oh, I see. It's one of the labels I've won at the office. It was Kirk Mason who invented it, unless I'm mistaken. But I'm not really made of snow.'

'No, I don't believe you are baby. You're made of everthing that's soft and — and cuddly and desirable.'

She laughed again, showing her white teeth.

'Just like a teddy-bear?'

'I've never heard of a desirable teddy-bear. But then I was weaned pretty young. In fact I don't remember ever having a teddy-bear. But why stray from the point? You are a peach, Claire.'

'With a stone in the centre?'

Denton's hand firmed on her fingers. He could feel an exaggerated pulse-beat, but it could have been his own heart he felt thumping.

'You never know, Blake,' she answered slowly. 'It would depend on how deep you go, I guess.'

'I intend to go plenty deep, sister. You know something, Claire, honey, you intrigue me.'

'You know something else, big boy, you're practically stinking.'

'No, I'm not. Say, what do you think of that old goat, Hank? Really think, I mean?'

24

'He is our boss, Blake.'

'Of course he is. But he makes me sick the way he tried to fondle you.'

She made an airy gesture with her free hand.

'He's harmless.'

'Yeah. So is a Browning automatic rifle until you mess about with the trigger.'

He saw a shadow of annoyance flit over her features. She released her fingers, doing it gently and with a smile at her lips. She touched the burnished halo that was her hair.

'Dance time, Blake. Like to shake a leg?'

'Why not?'

She danced like a dream and he held her close to him, feeling the softness of her bosom pressing into him. His blood thickened and he brushed her cheek with his lips, murmuring as he did so, 'Oh, my!'

'You don't go out with many girls, Blake?'

'Of course I do. Hundreds and hundreds. I bring a different one home each night. Yes, sir, Claire baby, I'm a pretty vital guy.'

'Tough too, I'd say?'

He stared at her but she was smiling disarmingly.

'Once upon a time. You had to be tough to survive. But what am I saying? I knew some tough cookies and they didn't survive.'

'I see that you limp occasionally.'

'It's still noticable? I figured my leg was as good as new. But look, let's sample some other subject, huh? Would you like to get out of here? Would you like to go to the beach over Mount Palmer way?'

She shook her head. She stared into his eyes before laying it on his shoulder. He kissed her cheek again. It was oddly cool and she didn't seem to mind.

The music ran down and started up almost immediately in jive number. Denton groaned.

'If that's how you want it, mister, count me out.'

'Me too,' Claire laughed.

They went back to their table and Denton signalled for a waitress.

'Remember that you're going to be driving shortly, big boy.'

'Hell yes. You made me forget. You have a capacity for making a guy forget things, Claire. You're sweet, you know.'

'So are you, Blake.'

The waitress arrived but he apologized and said they didn't want anything. The heat in the dimly-lit room was beginning to reach Denton, despite the air-conditioning. He offered the girl a cigarette and lit one for himself.

'It really is a joke,' he said.

'What is?' She puffed at her cigarette, blew the smoke at the ceiling.

'You and me together in this way,' he said. 'Old Kirk would fall down dead. Old Hank would have an apoplectic fit.'

'He is our boss, Blake.'

'So you keep on insisting. He'd still have a fit if he could see us together. Has he ever asked you out?'

'Once or twice.' She was looking at her wristwatch and seemed to be thinking of something else.

'You ever go out with the old gopher?'

'Once or twice.'

It took him on the raw. 'Hey!' he cried. 'You're kidding, aren't you? But no, you're not. Well, well! I'll be a grasshopper's uncle. But surely he didn't — '

'Let's drop it, Blake,' she said sharply. 'I'm a diplomat, whatever else I am. But I'm not an easy lay if it's what you think I am.'

'I didn't think you were.'

'Then drop it, will you?'

'Sure, sure.' The drinks had made his head muzzy. Had he been his usual alert self he wouldn't have barged on. 'But tell me something for nothing, baby. That five-spot on the floor. Why did you do it?'

'It was Mr Otis'.'

'Like blazes it was! Oh, don't ice up on me, Claire. We're pals now. You must have had some reason for doing it. I simply want to know what it was.'

'You're wrong,' she said stiffly. 'You imagine I was putting cheese at a trap to catch a mouse?'

'How about a rat?' he grinned. 'King-size. Like in me, honey. You wondered if I had the makings of a thief, didn't you? How did I come out of the game?'

She said nothing for a minute. She

looked slightly confused and unsure of herself. She glanced at her wristwatch again.

'It's after midnight, Blake. I'd better get off home. You too. If I don't get my sleep ration I'll have a headache come the dawn.'

He realized he'd gone further than was advisable, and if he wasn't careful she might drop him like a hot potato. It would be a pity if she were to draw the curtains on their relationship just when it seemed most promising.

In spite of his claim to the effect that he was capable of handling his car she insisted on taking the wheel on the journey back to her apartment in St Ann's Avenue.

'Okay, Claire, okay. I never argue with a lady. Well, not very often,' he added with a croaking laugh. 'I meet so few ladies in my line of business.'

She smiled at him but said nothing. She drove without haste until they were over the bad road and halting on the asphalt area that fronted the apartment block.

This was where she poured her pail of water on his ambitions, he told himself as she switched off the motor. She didn't, though. She said he might come up for a cup of coffee if he felt like it.

'Feel like it! Honey-chile, I figured you would never ask me.'

He hummed gently on the way into the vestibule, taking her arm and leering blatantly in the muted lighting.

'You better know what you're doing, Miss Paige. Away from a typewriter and a sheaf of invoices I do get the craziest urges.'

'Not with me you won't, little wolf. I put a man in hospital once with a single blow to a sensitive section of his anatomy.'

'What a surprise you've turned out to be! Still, a bit of opposition has a spice of its own.'

They had the elevator to themselves and he brought her into his arms and kissed her. She could try crippling him now and get it over with if she had a mind to. She just clung to him briefly, then pushed him off.

'You have been warned, little wolf.'

'This side has got a bum eardrum. Better try the other side.'

'Crazy is the word.'

The apartment was modern and the decor strictly feminine, without having too many frills and flounces. In the lounge Denton flung his hat at a chair. It missed and fell on the rug. He laughed and the girl stared curiously at him.

'What's with the merriment?' he said, slipping his arms about her waist and bringing her body tightly against him. 'I behave like a comedian?'

'You've certainly got two facets to your character, Blake. Two at least. The one you show in the office and the one you show in your recreation periods.'

'Three,' he told her and touched the tip of her nose with his lips. 'At least.'

'Oh. How come?' She struggled to free herself but it was a half-hearted effort and he paid no attention.

'You saw that one as well.'

'I don't understand.'

'I picked up your five bucks, baby. It makes me some kind of thief. This proves it.'

He claimed her mouth, revelling in the softness of her and in the awakening hunger he sensed being triggered. Her lips had been cool, but heat was streaking into them in soaring response.

She broke away at last, straightening her dress and running her fingers over her hair. Her eyes fought with him.

'Whew! Where do you get all that potential?'

'Clean living and early nights,' he chuckled. 'It's marvellous what it does for a guy.'

'And calamitous what it can do for a girl. Come into the kitchen and I'll make you coffee.'

They were sitting on stools, drinking it, when the telephone burred. Claire jumped up and laid her cup on the table. She frowned as she excused herself and passed through to the lounge. By listening closely Denton could hear what she said even though she spoke in a lowered voice.

'Yes, yes . . . I know. No, not tonight . . . Well, I'm busy, you see, and — No, I won't forget. Another day or so. Oh, all right. If you must you must.'

She said goodbye and replaced the receiver on its rest. It was several minutes before she rejoined Denton. The frown was still on her brow and there was an odd little gleam in her eye.

'Not bad news, I hope,' he said casually. He had finished with his coffee and brought cigarettes from his pocket.

'No, no. Nothing like that, Blake. But look, I'm afraid we're going to have to call it a day.'

It was that way then. Some guy had been calling her. She had been careful enough not to mention any name on the phone. Perhaps she was due another visitor and that was why she wanted rid of him.

He gave her a cigarette, held his lighter for her. The green, hazel-flecked eyes clashed with his own.

'Okay,' he said, coming off his stool.

'I'm sorry, Blake.' She puffed at the cigarette, blew the smoke at the ceiling.

'Don't worry. It's been great fun.' He went through to the lounge and picked up his hat. She had lifted it from the floor and laid it on the chair he'd aimed at. At the outside door she touched his arm with her spread fingers. He turned to look at her.

'Another evening, Blake?'

'I can't wait,' he grinned, bending over to kiss her. Then he went out and closed the door behind him.

Down on the street he unlocked the Volkswagen and slid on to the driving seat. He was moving off when an idea occurred to him, and instead of continuing along the street he spun the car in a circle that took him away from the asphalt forecourt and put him on the opposite side of the road. He switched off the engine and lights and waited.

Twenty minutes later a car came jouncing over the unmade road, spewing dust from its wheels and making dancing arcs in the air with its headlamps. The car drove on to the forecourt and stopped. A man climbed out. He was tall and compactly-built, dressed in dark clothes and wearing a snapbrim hat. Denton couldn't see him clearly enough to be able to recognize him again. Anyhow, he might have nothing to do with Claire. Denton knew he was only kidding himself. She had been talking to a man. She had wanted to postpone his visit till another time, but he'd insisted on coming to see her tonight.

Who? It didn't matter a curse who. She was a dame. She enjoyed a frolic outside working hours. Who was he to sit in judgment on her?

He watched the man pass into the lobby and go from view. He reached for the ignition switch, but then paused. He reached into the glove compartment instead and brought out a flashlight. Assured that the coast was clear, he got out of the Volkswagen and crossed the wide road to the parked car.

It was a shiny Olds, and Denton was at the driving side window and about to stab the flash at the steering column to see if he could read the licence tag when another car rolled into the avenue, red roof-light winking. A police prowl car.

He hastily back-tracked to his own car, shut himself in, and drove off through the darkness.

3

During the next two days Claire hardly glanced in his direction. It was as if she had stepped out of her deep-freeze unit, looked around her, decided that playing hard to get was her particular game, and gone back on ice again.

Her behaviour was baffling to Denton. It beat him why she had thawed to the degree of going out with him and making up to him in the way she had done and then dropped him like a stocking that hadn't worn too well.

She made sure they were never alone in the office together, and when the day's work was over she kept Hank Otis at her desk on some pretext so that Denton would be forced to leave in front of her.

He called her apartment on those two evenings, but could get no reply to his ring. Finally, he said the hell with her and concentrated on the garage he was going to have one day.

He was surprised when, on Friday, she hustled out of the building on his heels as he walked to the car park to pick up his Volkswagen.

'Hi there, Blake,' she said in a voice that was pitched for his ears alone.

'Oh, hi,' Denton grunted, scarcely breaking his stride. 'You haven't been missing five-dollar bills.'

'That isn't fair, Blake,' She looked over her shoulder to see if they were being observed. Denton saw the tail-end of Kirk Mason's car vanishing up the street. Sally Baines was seated at Kirk's side.

'All's fair in love and war, Miss Paige,' Denton said curtly. 'I was all for making love but obviously you're a war-monger of the first water.

'Okay,' she said shortly and walked away from him.

He called after her. 'Wait.'

She came back slowly and stood in front of him.

'Yes, Blake? Can we kiss and make up?'

'Not here,' he said with a faint smile bending his lips. 'Your reputation would take a beating. What are you doing this evening?'

'Not much,' she said and spread her hands. 'How about you?'

'Not much either,' he said and grinned. 'But look, honey, I'm not so well-versed in the ways of temperamental people. How do I know that an Arctic gale won't commence blowing between now and six-thirty?'

'Because I've been in touch with the weather experts. They say the situation stands fine and fair.'

'That I'll buy. With suitable reservations.' His grin broadened. 'Six-thirty then?'

'I'll be ready and waiting, Blake. Be seeing you, big boy.'

He was still puzzled as he drove to a diner and ate a meal before driving on home to his place. Now she wants me, now she doesn't, he reflected bleakly. Had it to do with the guy who rang her the other night and then appeared in his car? It was possible. The guy had been a straw in her hair, a bent spoke in her wheel. Now she had got rid of the straw and straightened out the bent spoke, so she was back on the open market again.

He didn't like the idea a lot, but there was nothing he could do about it. He could dump her, of course, see she stayed in the context of the stuffy office where they both worked. But that direction wasn't for fun. Underneath everything the dame had potential, and he admitted to a fascination for the way it might unfold.

He was pressing on her doorbell at six-thirty. As before, Claire was ready to step out with him. This evening she wore a natty tan outfit that hugged her marvellous figure and went well with her colouring and hair.

They had dinner at the same restaurant and Denton suggested they visit at a different nightspot. The *Hurdy Gurdy* was interesting, he told her, but she shook her head and he waited for her to make her own choice.

'It's too nice an evening to stay inside, Blake. I was thinking in terms of a drive in the fresh air. We could go as far as the coast. It's only an hour's drive. We could stop at Signal Beach for a while.'

'Super,' he smiled. 'Why didn't I think of it myself. But I never knew your were a fresh air fiend.'

The drive was made through the rosy glow of a picture-book sunset. There was a bar and grill on the beach, where they had a few drinks, then they went walking on the wet sand with the tide receding and the dying sun turning the rippling waves into a corrugated mirror.

'Boy, oh boy!' Denton breathed. 'Me for the great out of doors after this experience. Say, listen to those gulls . . . '

They listened to the gulls. They dragged their feet in the sand, drawing figures and patterns. A breeze sprang up and wafted coolly against their cheeks. On a rocky promontory they sank down to rest and Denton brought the girl into his arms. Her kiss was honest and demanding, and Denton's senses reeled out in concord with the muted drum and beat of the sea.

A moment later she was pushing him away from her. His hand had been at the lush softness of her left breast and her breathing had become shallow and rapid.

'Here!' she panted, staring at him through the shadows. 'That's too potent for safety, Blake.'

He sat and stared back at her, touching his bruised lips with the tip of his tongue.

'There's a spice to living dangerously, honey. What are you afraid of?'

'I don't know.' Her eyes were large and luminous in the darkness. 'Involvement, perhaps.'

A vision of the tall man in the snapbrim hat touched Denton's thoughts. He brushed it away.

'You don't want to get involved? It's why you pull that shell around you? It's why you keep yourself on ice for most of the time?'

'Snow Queen,' she said and laughed. 'Kirk Mason may have got something.'

'Maybe. Mason doesn't know what I know, though. He has never held his hands to the slow flame burning underneath. I met his wife once. She nearly put me off women for good.'

'Then there is no steady mate waiting behind a bedroom door?'

'Not for me, baby. Not for me.'

'You wouldn't want it, either?'

'What are you trying to do, Miss Paige — perform a psychoanalysis effort on me?'

'It could be interesting.'

'But hardly rewarding.' He brought out his cigarettes and gave her one. He lit it with his lighter and then lit one for himself. She puffed and blew the smoke skyward in that habit that would be hard to break. She was looking out to sea now, apparently listening to the battling of the receding waves. The sky was a dull, drab curtain with a few stars twinkling valiantly like sequins hoping to transform a dowdy dress.

'Have you thought of marriage, Blake?'

'Sure, I have,' he said without hesitation. 'The same way I think about strychnine as a whisky chaser.'

'Not for you, huh?'

'I'm only joking, Claire,' he added seriously. 'I guess it might be okay. But this is so sudden. I mean — '

'Oh, stop it,' she laughed. 'I'm not proposing marriage to you. I was merely trying to look at life from your angle.'

'Take a word of sound advice, honey, and spare yourself the bother. Look. What would I do with a wife? Put her out to the office in the morning and tell her to keep on asking for raises? Well, how can you keep pace with the cost of living if you don't keep on asking for raises.'

'Rises.'

'Raises, rises. You'd like to be married to a guy who could keep you at home to mend his socks and raise — or rise — his children.'

'Raise.'

'Yeah, well whatever it is. But it's what you'd like to do if you were married to a guy?'

'I suppose so.' She took a drag from her cigarette and flipped it off the promontory. It spun briefly like a firefly and was swallowed in the darkness.

'You don't suppose so. You know. How would I feel being latched to a girl who had to put up with a frustrated old jerk like Hank Otis, who spends the whole day figuring what year it will be when he gets to taking a nip out of your behind?'

She laughed again. It was a hilarious

explosion of mirth that triggered off an anger in Denton.

'It isn't funny at all,' he snarled.

'I know.'

'Then you have your answer. I wouldn't wish it on a dame who was my worst enemy, never mind — '

'Who, Blake?'

'Hell, you. Who else?'

'You don't have to get yourself a head of steam,' she chided 'I didn't propose to you. You didn't propose to me.'

'Meaning I couldn't? If I did you wouldn't accept? Please, Miss Paige! An elementary move for any woman is to find out which side her bread is buttered. Old Hank could provide lots of butter. He must be stinking with it.'

'Marry for money? Well . . . when you come to think of it . . . '

'Sure! It could get better the more you think of it. A load of moolah in the bank. A fat insurance policy. A gink who's got at least one of his flat feet in a six by three plot. Now there's a pretty picture if you're in a creative mood.'

'I'm still interested in you, Blake. What

are you going to do with your life? For how long are you going to type invoices for two dozen walking, talking dolls?'

'You're just kidding, aren't you?'

'No, I'm not kidding. But then, you might not have any ambitions. I couldn't blame you. A man's life is his own to do with what he likes.'

'Wisdom simply drools out of you, doesn't it?' He flung his butt away and lit another cigarette. The tide was right out now and the sand flats were a dull grey that deepened to blackness seaward. More stars were flickering in the sky. The breeze was freshening and the heat stored up in the rocks had evaporated. He wanted to bring the woman into his arms and forget about his future. Then he decided he would let her see that he wasn't completely lacking in ambition.

He told her about the garage he was going to start, how he was saving steadily towards that end. She listened to him talk without interrupting him. Finally she spoke.

'How long will it take you, Blake?'

'Oh, hell, I don't know. Another year or

so. But I'm up to my chin in that office. I might make a break soon and take the plunge with what I have. I can sink or swim, according to the way the cards fall.'

'Twenty thousand dollars would help you achieve your ends?'

'What?' he cried while a sharp file traced a scratching course over his spine. 'Are you nuts, Claire?'

'Forget it,' she said abruply. She rose to her feet and straightened out the short skirt over her strong, rounded thighs. 'It's getting cold. We'd better head back to the car.'

He rose with her while a dozen questions stormed through his mind. What had she meant by that crack? Was it a crack? Had she been simply joking, playing at pie in the sky? He didn't know. He couldn't bring himself to ask her. Certainly he wanted nothing to do with charity in any guise or form.

They walked to the bar where Denton had a Scotch on ice and the girl had a pink gin. He sensed a slight change in her demeanour, in the very atmosphere that surrounded them. She seemed thoughtful to the point of moodiness, but he said nothing to jar her out of it.

On the journey back to town she relaxed somewhat, reminiscing over Hank Otis and Jack Rhodes.

'They say they started on a shoestring and even that was badly worn. But they must have worked their guts out.'

'Where did it get them?' Claire reasoned. 'Hank has ulcers and a frustration. Jack Rhodes is as jumpy as a cat — lynx type, that is. Oh, it shows, Blake. It really shows.'

'I'm not going to work my guts out,' Denton said grimly. 'I shouldn't be alive at all.'

'You do say!' she cried, bitten by curiosity. 'Your spell in the army?'

'Yeah. Look, drop it, baby. But I've got this thing about living on borrowed time. No. Time bought for me by my buddies.'

'Crazy, Blake, crazy,' she murmured and snuggled up to him. He looped his arm about her shoulders and kissed her on the forehead.

Winding their way through the suburbs he asked her if she would care to stop at

47

his place. She said she would prefer to go to her own apartment. They reached the block at length and went up in the elevator to the seventh floor. Inside, Claire said she would fix coffee, but Denton was for crushing her to him and kissing her fiercely.

She responded for a moment and then wormed free of him, telling him the beach air must have had alcohol in it.

'You can't spin me that line tonight, honey. I'm as sober as a judge and I know what I'm doing.'

'Even so, Blake, I want to be sure I know what I'm doing.'

She made for the kitchen and he let her go. He sat in an easy chair in front of the TV and worked the remote control for a while, switching from station to station. Just then he was thinking of the tall stranger once more and wondering if he really had been calling on her. It would be an easy thing to ask her, but he didn't.

She brought in coffee and moved to the large studio couch when she had served him. He studied her for a few seconds and went across to join her.

48

'We could always build some kind of wall.'

'Don't misunderstand me, Blake,' she said with a gravity which impressed him. With her left hand she straightened out her skirt on her knees. He let an amused smile pucker the corner of his mouth.

'Message received loud and clear, lady. Play it safe we will. How long have you been grinding at *Advance*?'

'Two years.'

'I figured it must have been longer. Like it?'

'A girl has got to do something for a living.'

'Do I detect a note of resignation? Then you aren't exactly enchanted with the job?'

'A person is seldom enchanted with what it is necessary to do to earn his daily bread.'

'I'll tell you what we could do, baby. You and me together. We could pool our resources and take a plane out to Miami. Have a positive ball. Live like a king and queen for a couple of months — or a

49

couple of weeks. The notion appeal to you?'

She laughed softly.

'One minute you pretend you're a dedicated soberhead, the next that you're incorrigibly reckless.'

He sipped some of his coffee and shrugged.

'What else can I do but play pretending games? As soon as I get too close to you you turn on the chill. Some other guy in the background?'

He suspected her gaze shadowed momentarily, but it could have been in his imagination. She shook her head.

'No one.'

'Lone wolf, huh? Just like me. What about this twenty thousand bucks you mentioned?'

She started then right enough. She laid her coffee on the small table at her side, rose and took a turn over the room. Baffled, Denton placed his cup down also and went to catch her shoulders.

She spun, the red hair spilling about her shoulders in a sparkling cloud. Her eyes were large and anxious and the red lips lay open in invitation. Denton claimed them. He ground his own mouth down hard on them. She moaned and tried to break away from him. He held her all the tighter, his fingers travelling from her shoulders to her waist, to the soft rounded contours of her hips.

She writhed and moved her thighs against him, then panted into the heat of his breathing.

'No, Blake, no . . . '

'Why not?' he demanded hoarsely. 'Do you want to remain an iceberg until you're an old woman?'

He lifted her up in his arms, carried her to the bedroom as though she weighed no more than a rag doll. Once through the doorway she surrendered the last vestige of restraint.

He didn't have to rip the clothes from her. She stripped herself, revealing a ripe body that tapered from high, full breasts to narrow waist, then widened to firm, solid hips and smoothed off into rich, strong, cream-fleshed thighs.

She smiled at him in a queer fashion, eyes closed, head held poised on the slender column of her neck. Her body arched and when she spoke her voice seemed to come from a long distance off.

'Where are you, Blake? Where are you . . . '

4

They clung together in the soft, musky darkness. Denton shifted slightly to reach for his cigarettes, but she pulled his arm back across her body. She burrowed in to him, making little sounds of laughter in her throat. Her hair trickled on his face.

'What's so funny?'

'I don't know. I'm not really laughing, Blake. I just feel good. There isn't any law against feeling good?'

'None that I've heard of.'

She kissed the side of his neck, her teeth catching the skin there and nibbling at it.

'Take it easy,' he said. 'You might eat me all up in a single meal, and then where would I be?'

'In my stomach, darling.' She laughed again. He never ceased wondering at her laughter. Miss Paige had never laughed in his experience. She was two people. She had a split-personality. When she went to the office in the morning she left this part of her at home, the soft part of her, the living, aware part of her. It was a machine that went to the office in the mornings, albeit a beautiful, smoothly-functioning one. He tried to figure out when she discovered she was two people.

He told her what he was thinking and she laughed hilariously. Her laughter was so loud he had to cut it off with his mouth. They crawled towards their private world again. Time passed. On the next occasion Denton stirred he took his cigarettes from his jacket pocket and gave the girl one. They lay on their backs in the intimate shadows and smoked. Below them traffic rumbled dimly on the street, bounced across the unmade road.

'You were kidding, weren't you?' he said to her.

'Of course I was. I wouldn't eat you. I'm not a cannibal. Here! I could be a cannibal!'

'Knock it off, Claire,' he said brusquely. 'You know what I'm talking about.'

'Do I?' she murmured innocently, twisting her head to look at the dark outline of his profile. His chest rose and fell slowly. The tip of his cigarette glowed to a bright crimson as he inhaled.

'Twenty thousand, you said. It was a gag, wasn't it? Have you got twenty thousand bucks?'

'Me? Lordy, no, Blake! I've got a thousand dollars in savings.'

'Then it was a gag, Claire? But don't think I'd take any money off you. I was just wondering.'

'No, it's real right enough,' she said reflectively. 'But — but it was only a joke, really. It doesn't belong to me. It doesn't belong to a rich uncle or aunt I've got stashed away in the country. I don't have a living relation in the world.'

He thought of the tall man in the snapbrim hat, but he didn't mention him. He was interested in the twenty thousand dollars. It was there or it wasn't. 'Where? How do we get it?'

She told him.

'You would have to steal it.'

'Oh.'

He swung his naked frame to the floor and ran his hand across the crisp, prickly crewcut of his hair. She lay and watched him mash his cigarette butt into an ashbowl. He stood there for a moment in the darkness, gazing down at her. From this distance it was impossible to see her eyes. He heard her light breathing, distinguished the twin mounds of her breasts.

He gathered up his clothes and went into the bathroom, and a few seconds later she heard the sound of the shower. She finished her cigarette and leaned over to the nightstand on her side of the bed, dropping the dogend into a tray.

Denton left the bathroom after a while and moved down the passage. He was making for the kitchen. Claire lay back and stared at the ceiling, her forehead puckered in thought. He had dropped his cigarette pack on his side of the bed and she switched on the nightlight to find it.

She was engrossed in her thoughts when he pushed open the door, carrying a tray of coffee cups, sugar and cream. He was dressed in his shoes, pants and shirt, the shirt collar slack and tieless.

'That smells great, Blake. I've got a

bottle in a cupboard if you want to spike it.'

'You want yours spiked?'

'No, thanks.'

'Neither do I.'

He fixed the bed cover to take the tray, then sat down on the edge of the bed and handed her a cup. She added sugar and cream to hers but Denton had his coffee black and unsweetened. She knew he had been thinking deeply just as she had been thinking.

'What would you do if we had twenty grand between us, Claire?'

'But — but I was only joking, Blake.'

'Then it couldn't be got at? You were just making talk to heat the air?'

'No — no, I wasn't.'

'It could be got at?' he persisted tautly.

'Yes, I suppose so. But yes, there isn't much doubt about it. All you would need is a cool nerve . . . '

'I've got a cool nerve. You didn't tell me where the dough is. But I can guess. *Advance?*'

She nodded slowly, her gaze dubious over the rim of her cup. They stared at each other and said nothing. Denton went on sipping at his coffee. Along the passage somewhere a door slammed. On the street a heavy night transport truck rumbled past.

'But it's silly to even consider it, Blake.'

'Is it? How do you know it's silly? How can you say it's silly? Only, how come twenty thousand greenbacks are stored at the warehouse? Jack Rhodes and Hank Otis have never heard of a bank?'

'It isn't there now,' she explained to him. 'Not at this minute. But it will be there. I know it will be there.'

'And we could snatch it?'

'Forget it.' She made a dismissal gesture and drank her coffee. Her hands trembled slightly on the cup, he noticed. She looked up at him and laughed nervously. 'It was an idea that came into my head, Blake. It seemed to pop in from nowhere five minutes after I learned what was in the wind. I said to myself, 'What could you do with that sort of money, Claire?' I could see myself taking off from Maxwell and that dreary grind. First I decided I would go to Europe. You know?

France, Italy, England. Those places . . . '

'With the cops racing after you for a chance to breathe down your neck? That would be crazy, Claire.'

'Of course it would. I would have to be more subtle. More discreet.' Her eyes danced recklessly on him. 'You see how you could become a criminal if you tried hard enough, Blake. It's a simple matter of conditioning yourself, telling yourself that you are right and they are wrong. But that isn't enough, either. Cunning comes into it as well. You must realize the danger of playing it too wild, or too close, at the other end of the scale — '

'You're a pretty smart baby, Claire,' he complimented her. She ignored the interruption. She went on with enthusiasm. 'I would pack it all in a suitcase and hide the suitcase in a safe place. Then I would turn up for my work as usual the following morning. I would play my part to the hilt, registering astonishment, then horror. If Mr Otis wished to weep on my shoulder I would let him — '

'Nip your behind?'

'He could nip it for twenty thousand

dollars worth,' she cried gaily. She pointed a finger at Denton, her concentration remaining with her tale. 'The police would come, of course. They would put all of us against a wall and ask their questions. They could ask questions until they developed blue faces. I would wait for a month, for two months, for six months — until the heat blew over and the police and the partners Otis and Rhodes had faced the inevitable conclusion that the robbery was planned and executed by a gang of professionals, and — '

Denton bent over and shook her hard.

'Knock it off,' he said harshly. 'I'm not laughing at it, Claire. It isn't a joke. It's something to think about seriously.'

She gaped at him.

'You would do it, Blake?'

'Why not? But stick to the facts, Claire. The essentials. And before you begin, tell me one thing I've got to be absolutely clear on. What would you do if we got this money — if I got it? If I pulled off the snatch successfully?'

She sobered, pushing a tendril of hair

from her face. His shaking had caused some of her coffee to be spilled. It had dribbed on to her breasts and trickled down into the deep cleft between them. He took the cup from her and flung her a towel to mop up the coffee. She met the fire in his eyes.

'You really aren't kidding, Blake?' she said slowly. 'You are on the level?'

'Could it be done?' he snapped.

'Yes . . . I guess it could. I — I carry a key to the front door of the warehouse. I know the combination of Mr Otis' safe. It's where the money will be kept. It's where he kept it the last time. He collected it from the bank in the afternoon — just before the bank closed for the day. He gave Kirk the gun he has for his own protection. Kirk went to the bank with him in his car. On their return Mr Otis locked the money in his safe. Then — then when Mr Waterman called promptly at nine the next morning with the watches — '

'Waterman? Watches? What do I know about Waterman and watches? Tell me.'

She told him. It had happened twice

before. The man called Waterman had contacted Hank Otis by phone. Claire received the call and then put Hank on. Hank Otis trusted her completely and she knew what was taking place. The consignment of watches was stolen or smuggled. It came as a surprise to him that the partners would stoop to illegal practices? Denton was only mildly surprised, knowing the world and the ways of the world.

'What you're saying is that Hank and Waterman make their deals by phone. Nothing is committed to writing. The basis of the deals is that Waterman arrives with his consignment of watches and gets paid in ready cash. No cheques, no strings of any nature which might incriminate him?'

'It's all there is to it, Blake. I've never given it a thought before. Well, why should I? I get a generous salary. Mr Otis trusts me implicitly. It never occurred to me to tell the police or anyone else.'

'I see,' Denton grunted, his thoughts racing. He lifted the cigarette pack and fingered one to his lips. He lit it and considered the girl for a long time. Yes, it could be swung without much trouble, he reckoned. Claire had the front door key and knew the combination of the safe. That should make it easy. Real easy. Still, there was a snag to be examined. The very fact of her carrying a key and being in a position where she could open Otis' safe could make her number one suspect when the cops came on to the scene.

'You would be the first person the cops would latch on to, honey. You realize that?'

She nibbled at her underlip for a moment, but her gaze stayed fixedly on his own as she nodded.

'It's understandable. But I'd have everything on my side, Blake. Mr Otis trusts me, as I said. He would never suspect me of robbing him in a hundred years. I'm sure I could weather it. It's you I'm thinking of, darling. If you made a slip, left a fingerprint behind — '

'Don't worry,' Denton said grimly. 'I wouldn't leave anything behind. But here. What about Kirk? I wouldn't want the guy getting in trouble. He's got enough trouble at home as it is. Can he open the safe?'

Claire shook her head.

'I'm the only one besides Mr Otis who has the combination.'

'Rhodes would have it?'

'Oh, yes, he would. But suspicion would hardly fall on Mr Rhodes.'

What matter if it did, Denton thought fleetingly. It couldn't be better, he decided. When they had the money they would stash it out of sight, sit on it for a month or so, and then, when the cops had given up searching, he and Claire would hit out together for distant parts. Not together, but they would come together eventually. He would marry her if she said the word. It wouldn't be difficult falling in love with her. He imagined he was deeply in love with her at this minute.

What about that stranger who had called on her? Who was he? Had he called on her? He had no way of knowing for sure, and until he did know for sure there was no valid reason for challenging her.

'That would let Kirk out,' he said. 'Leave just three people that the cops could point a finger at. You think you could weather it, and I bet you could, too, baby. What kind of safe is it?'

She told him the make and the model. It was at least fifteen years of age, and she explained how the tumblers were so worn almost any amateur could open it in an hour or so.

'That makes it all the sweeter, Claire,' Denton said happily. Already the excitement of the proposed venture was taking possession of him. It would be an absolute cinch. It would be a walkover. Planned with care and carried through with the right amount of skill and nerve, he couldn't see a thing to trip them up. Of course, in the final analysis, the success of the project would rest on the girl's nerve. If she bent beneath police questioning the whole effort would go up in a puff of smoke. She seemed to grasp something of the thoughts running through his head.

'Don't worry about me, Blake. Just concentrate on your own part.'

'When is the money going to be in the safe?'

'Six days from today. Thursday.'

'You're perfectly certain of this? Otis and Waterman have been cooking up another deal?'

'I'm certain enough. Mr Otis told me all about it. It has got to the stage where he discusses his deals with Mr Waterman as though they are nothing to be ashamed of.'

'So, the dough would be in the safe Thursday night, and Waterman would turn up with his consignment of watches first thing Friday morning?'

'That's right, Blake. If a snag crops up in the meantime I'd learn about it as soon as Mr Otis would.'

He told her to get out of bed and dress and come into the living room.

'It's impossible to think straight with you lying there as you are,' he grinned.

'Off you go then,' she smiled at him. 'Draw another cup of coffee and have it ready for me.'

They talked for another hour, going over the matter in detail. It had occurred to Blake that the partners might employ a watchman he had never heard of. There was no watchman, Claire assured him. The building was completely empty from when Hank Otis or Jack Rhodes locked up at night until eight-thirty the following morning.

'You give me your key,' he said.

'What, now? But I might need it between now and next Thursday, Blake.'

'You won't need it tomorrow, will you? Tomorrow the shebang closes down for the weekend.'

'Well, all right.' Reluctantly she got her purse and brought out a fob of keys. She selected one of them and passed it over. 'What are you planning?'

'Tomorrow morning I'll take a drive somewhere and have a matching key made. I won't do it here in town. I'll drive to some other town. Chandler or Hickson. I won't tell you which so you won't have to worry about it.'

'Smart thinking, Blake. Of course. But remember to get rid of it immediately after you use it.'

'You don't have to tell me, honey. My faculties are on edge. At the beginning of the week I'll do a dry run on the act. It'll give me a chance to get the feel of the place. Now, we've reached the point where I enter the warehouse building on Thursday night, open the safe, grab the twenty grand, and make it back to my car. Where would be the best place to leave the dough? It would be risky bringing it to your apartment, and it would be as risky taking it to mine. The cops are bound to search. Where then?'

'It's got to be a spot where nobody would dream of looking, Blake.'

'You can say that again. But where?'

They thought about it for a while, discussed this idea and that, discarded all of them as impractical. Then Claire suggested Fosset's woods. The woods lay a good ten miles to the north of Maxwell. Did he know how to get there? He did. He had taken a girl on a joyride to the woods one Sunday, but he didn't tell Claire so. Yes, Fosset's woods would serve. It was a deserted stretch of no-man's land. The turf was soft enough to enable him to dig a hole. He would choose a tree, mark it in some fashion, and dig a hole for the suitcase he would be carrying the money in. He must remember to buy a shovel.

They talked a little longer, drank a toast in Scotch to the success of their plan. Then, at twenty minutes after midnight, Denton kissed Claire Paige and left her apartment.

5

He prepared to drive to Chandler next morning to have the key made. At the last moment he decided he should take Claire with him, and when he had secured the key they could spend the day driving around together.

After drinking a cup of coffee he put a call through to the girl's apartment.

'Sorry, Blake,' she said. 'I've got my own plans cut and dried for the day. I'll be busy at the stores until noon at least. Then I'm going to drop in at a hairdressing salon where I've made an appointment.'

'It was just an idea,' he chuckled. 'I'm kind of getting used to your company. But it might be as well to sheer off from each other, especially in daylight.'

'Yes, it would, Blake. You never know which eagle eye is going to spot us.'

'What about this evening then?'

'I'll be here from about seven o'clock onwards.'

'Swell, baby. Expect me at seven o'clock.'

'Goodbye, darling,' Claire said in a whisper that set his pulse-beat throbbing. She broke the connection.

Of course, he thought, tooling the Volkswagen along the Chandler freeway. It could prove fatal if they were seen fraternizing when the girl was supposed to be an ice-box who hardly knew of his existence. The cops would quickly add one and one together next Thursday night — or Friday morning. They would smell a collusion, and while it wouldn't be damning evidence in itself, it could still make for an awkward situation.

Only, who would have seen them — Kirk Mason, treating his ever-loving to a day trip to Chandler? Not so likely, he reflected with a tight grin. Poor Kirk was tied to enough of his own trouble to keep him occupied. Sally Baines then? Old Hank? The bustling, get-there-in-front-of-everybody-else Jack Rhodes? Denton laughed to himself. No matter. The less he and Claire saw of each other in public the better.

When he began thinking seriously about the proposed robbery he was a little disappointed at the overall picture. It was a pity there wouldn't be fifty thousand dollars in Hank Otis' safe instead of twenty. He would be sticking his neck out for a paltry twenty thousand bucks. It wasn't a fortune. Far from it. But at least it was something, and he and Claire would make good use of it. With that amount he could get a modest garage going. He would be his own man for a change. He and Claire would get married. Settle down and raise kids.

'Maybe,' he murmured at the road ahead of him. 'How do I know what will pan out in the future. If we get our hands on the dough Claire might decide we ought to split and go our separate ways. But so what?'

He shrugged fatalistically. The sky was becoming overcast and a light drizzle was commencing to fall. Denton whistled shrilly through his teeth.

In Chandler he had no bother getting a duplicate key cut from the one Claire had given him. He slid the duplicate into his billfold and dropped Claire's into his pocket. Chandler was a one-horse burg and he didn't tarry in it for long.

Back home in Maxwell he had a yearning to see the girl. It was queer how one dame out of thousand could find a way under your skin. At two o'clock he rang her apartment but got no reply. He remembered the hair-dressing appointment. He remembered that he mustn't be seen going near Claire's place in daylight.

Yet, by six-thirty, he was approaching St Ann's Avenue in the Volkswagen. He parked amongst the other cars on the asphalt forecourt and rode up in the elevator. The elevator halted at the seventh floor and Denton stepped out of it. He was striding along the passage to reach Claire's door when he met a tall man heading for the elevator. The man was past him before something registered with Denton. A vague feeling of familiarity. He looked over his shoulder at the man who was waiting for the elevator to return. The man was staring at him. Even as Denton's eyes touched him the man switched his head.

Frowning, Denton continued to 714 and pressed the bell button. The door opened and Claire stood looking at him.

'Why, Blake . . . you're early . . . '

A hint of colour stained both her cheeks, but it quickly receded as she smiled, grasped his arm and led him on into the apartment.

She threw herself into his arms and kissed him. Her mouth was warm and moist, but Denton terminated the kiss abruptly. She was dressed in fetching shorts and a halter. Her hair fell about her shoulders in the educated waves that came by courtesy of the hairdressing salon. Her full breasts strained against the halter.

She peered into his set features.

'Blake, is anything wrong? You look as though you might have met a ghost.'

'Ghost?' he murmured and smiled thinly. 'The guy I met just now in the passage was no ghost, baby.'

'What guy, Blake?'

She seemed genuinely amazed and took a couple of steps away from him. She laughed a sharp, nervous laugh.

'Do you hear me, Blake — what guy?'

Suddenly he began to feel foolish. Just then she was the picture of startled innocence, and no woman could behave in this fashion except she was an accomplished actress. He gestured weakly with his hand. 'Forget it,' he said sheepishly. 'It was nothing.'

'No!' she panted, stepping to him and sinking her fingers into his coat-sleeve. 'There is something. I don't understand you. A man, you said. A guy. What guy?'

'I met him in the passage. I thought — Oh, look, honey, I don't know what the hell I thought. But nobody has been calling on you?'

'A man?' she cried, her eyes wide and angry. 'You figure I've been entertaining a man behind your back. Oh, Blake . . . ' Her laugh was harsh now. 'How could you?'

'Yeah, I know.' He shrugged again. He tried to bring her to him but she eluded him, pouting and walking to the far side of the room where she confronted him, hands on hips, white teeth gnawing at her red underlip.

'There are times when I fail to fathom your depths, Blake. What ever *did* give you the notion I was seeing someone else?'

'Jealousy, I guess.' He chuckled. 'Can't we forget it?'

'I'm not so sure that I should,' she said slowly. 'I've heard of jealous men, Blake. The things they can wish themselves into. The things they can do to a woman when they lose their heads.'

'But I haven't lost my head. I misconstrued, that's all. I'm apologizing. It's over and done with. Kaput. I'm sorry. It won't happen again.'

Her shoulders began to relax and a feeble smile caused her mouth to soften.

'Then I forgive you. But only this once, remember, I wouldn't dream of making a pact with a man I couldn't trust and who didn't trust me.'

'So it's dead and done with.' He walked towards her and she stood still until he caught her and wrapped his arms around her.

'Did you get the key?' she asked presently.

'Yeah, I did. I'd better give you back your own.'

'And you've no regrets, Blake? No last minute qualms? It isn't too late to back out if you have.'

'I'm not backing out, Claire. I'm a character used to making rapid decisions and sticking to them. I've made one and I'm staying with it. Everything will be fine just so long as you stick with me.'

'Try and pry me away from you, big boy,' she whispered against his mouth. 'Or let anyone else try and pry us apart. I'm going to fight for you. Tooth and nail. Do you hear me, Blake — tooth and nail. You've bought yourself an article that's going to be very hard to shake. I hope you realize that.'

'Howcome you talk so damn much?' he growled, folding her to him and covering her lips with his own.

* * *

They stayed together all Saturday and Sunday. Monday posed the challenges of grim reality. They coped well enough.

Claire slid back into her deep-freeze for the benefit of the office staff. Denton carried on with his work and didn't bother looking at her. By now he was hopelessly in love with Claire.

He was still slightly troubled. A small doubt remained at the back of his mind to nag at him and torment him. If only it had occurred to him on Saturday to make a check on those cars on the forecourt of the apartment building. But why should it have occurred to him? And even if the tall man wearing the snapbrim hat he had met in the passage was the same man he had seen driving up in the Olds, just what did it prove? That he lived in the apartment building? That he was in the habit of visiting someone living on the seventh floor?

By Wednesday he had forgotten the tall man. He had other things to occupy his thoughts. Tonight he was going to do his dry run in preparation for tomorrow night.

He was a little anxious at this juncture. His principles were anything but hide-bound, so it wasn't the ethics of the situation that bothered him. What bothered him was the idea of being caught, either in the act of robbery or afterwards. The notion of court proceedings followed by a term in prison filled him with a chill fear. He thought he might go mad if he were to be shut up for any length of time.

By midnight on Wednesday he had calmed his fears. His nerve — healthy and flexible as ever, came to his aid. He had rung Claire at eleven and said simply that he was going out later. Claire had pleaded with him to be careful and he had the feeling it wouldn't take much to persuade her to drop the project. He said he would be careful. She had given him the combination of Hank Otis' safe. He had been surprised to hear the combination had never been altered since the day the safe was installed.

He left his apartment at one-thirty, making the minimum of fuss driving off in his car. The beetle's exhaust was inclined to be somewhat noisy, and he had parked down the street, away from the front of his apartment house.

Twenty minutes later he was approaching Felmoy Avenue. Felmoy Avenue ran at a right-angle to Cable Street where the warehouse and offices of *Advance Mail Order* were located. Denton left his car at the corner of the avenue and walked into Cable Street. It was a matter of a scant hundred yards from the corner to the *Advance* building.

The street was poorly-lighted. It was strictly a business zone and wasn't much used by traffic after office hours. *Advance* was tucked between a merchandising outfit on the left and a travel agency on the right. The street seemed deserted as Denton halted at the front door of the warehouse and brought the key from his pocket.

There must have been a roughness to the freshly-cut edges, because the key felt too tight a fit. It required a strong twist to get the lock to yield, but it did yield. The door open, Denton glanced quickly about him. He froze when a car turned the corner of Felmoy and raced along Cable Street. Denton stood stock-still until the vehicle swept past. He entered the dark, fusty-smelling hallway and closed the door behind him.

By the pencil gleam of the flashlight he carried he showed himself past the ground floor offices, the warehouse itself where the stuff they sold was stored, the packing rooms. A flight of stairs was in front of him now and he went up them. He knew how many stairs there were; he knew the weakened steps that would creak underfoot. The creaks seemed to echo through the vast rambling building like thunder.

It was a revelation to discover how calm he was, how keenly his senses were strung. The only thing missing was the jungle fronds, the steamy heat, the automatic rifle clutched in his hands. He shrugged wryly, went on.

The office where he spent his working day was on the first floor, and the familiar atmosphere wafted about him. It was familiar and yet it was strange. He had never stood here before in the darkness, with nothing but a flashlight to point out the desks, the dusty chairs, the hooded typewriters. He picked a clear path to

Hank Otis' cubby-hole in the rear, wondering with a sharpening of pulse-beat if Hank kept his door locked and Claire had overlooked the fact.

The door opened with a low creak. In front of him was Hank's desk and chair; a bank of filing cabinets were on the left of the tiny room, the big ancient safe on the right. Denton focused the flash beam on the safe.

He was wearing rubber gloves that fitted his fingers with the snugness of a second skin. He had memorized the combination, and he stooped before the safe and worked the tumblers. A few seconds later the safe door swung open.

Denton played the fine beam on the contents. There were masses of documents, some tied with pieces of cord, others held together with stout elastic bands. There was a steel cash box that Denton brought out and opened. It held some loose change, a score of bills — singles and fives.

He closed the box and replaced it. He closed the door of the safe and jumbled the tumblers. Then he left the office, pulling the door shut behind him, and headed through the main office to the stairway. The same steps creaked beneath the weight of his feet. He breathed easier when he reached the street and peered both ways. He closed the big heavy door, drew the collar of his jacket about his neck, and set off rapidly to gain the corner of Cable and Felmoy.

* * *

Denton was on tenterhooks all through the following morning, wondering if things would go as Claire believed they would. The only contact he had had with her was by telephone from a pay booth before going home last night. He had roused her to say the stage was set. She knew what he meant. She had sounded more anxious than ever, but her anxiety was all for him, for his luck to hold and for his ultimate safety.

He had hoped to have a word with her at the lunch hour, but old Hank claimed her at the last moment and Kirk Mason told him to hustle it if they were going to dine together, as he was starving.

During the meal Denton was tempted to ask Kirk if he would be making a trip to the bank this afternoon with Hank Otis. He saw the danger of this in time. It would be something for Kirk to remember afterwards, when the police got round to questioning him. It was hardly likely that Kirk would think of him in terms of the robbery, but there was no point in running unnecesary risks. The best thing to do was wait and see.

On the resumption of work in the afternoon Claire took a phone call which necessitated bringing old Hank from his private lair. Denton glanced across to Claire's desk and attempted to catch her eye, but her head was bent over a ledger while Hank talked into the mouthpiece. The phone conversation finished, Hank dallied to talk with the girl for a while, his right hand resting lightly at her waist. He could take those calls as easily in his own office, but apparently he preferred to make the most of every opportunity to paw around Claire.

At three o'clock, Hank, wearing his

black derby and holding a briefcase beneath one arm, emerged from his den. Watching him furtively, Denton felt a lurch in his chest. This was it, he told himself. Hank was going to summon Kirk and take him to the bank.

He could have fallen off his chair when Otis halted at his desk.

'Busy, Blake?'

'Busy enough, Mr Otis,' Denton said with a feeble smile. 'Is there anything I can do for you?'

'Yes, there is, Blake. Kirk is tied up with important letters. You were in the army. You can handle a gun. I want you to come to the bank with me. Matter of form,' he said with a humorous cackle. 'Let that stuff be till you get back.'

'Sure.' Denton rose and accepted the snubnosed .38 automatic that was extended to him. He checked it was on safety before putting it into his pocket. On their way out of the office he glanced at Claire's desk. Claire cast a quick look at him and lowered her eyes to her typewriter.

On the street a cab was drawn up at the

door. Denton saw Hank Otis on the back seat and slid in beside him.

'The First National Bank,' Hank directed the cabbie.

He nodded briefly, shifting his gum from one side of his mouth to the other, and started the motor.

Otis made trivial conversation on the way to the bank. He made no reference to his mission. He wanted to draw out Denton about the army but Denton kept switching the subject.

Denton accompanied Hank into the bank and stood beside him while the money was counted and passed over.

'Check it, Blake. I'm too slow at counting money.'

Denton counted the contents of each bundle and then gave the bundle to Otis to stow in the briefcase.

'That makes twenty thousand, Mr Otis,' he said finally.

'That's what it's supposed to make,' Hank cackled. 'Some of these guys prefer cash to a cheque,' he added off-handedly. 'You've got to humour them, I guess. But it could be dangerous, Blake.'

'I guess so,' Denton responded thickly. 'Shall we go?'

They went out to the cab waiting in the sunshine, Hank Otis leading the way and Denton covering him, right hand stuck in the pocket of his jacket.

On their return to the main office Hank took the gun from Denton, thanked him, and went into his cubbyhole with the briefcase.

When Denton sat down at his desk he glanced over at Claire. She was watching in her strip of mirror and their eyes met. Denton fancied she smiled slightly.

6

Work finished for the day, he drove to the market quarter of Maxwell and bought a short-handled shovel at a store specializing in garden implements. As well as this he bought a six feet by six square of polythene. The polythene was to wrap the suitcase that would contain the twenty thousand dollars before burying it in Fosset's woods. There was no knowing how long they would have to be patient before lifting the suitcase and making use of the money. Whilst he was at the gardening store Denton also purchased a second pair of rubber gloves, just in case he happened to get a tear in the pair he already had.

A suitcase had been stowed in the trunk of his car since morning, and he put the shovel and the spare pair of gloves in the trunk, wrapped up in the polythene.

He had a meal before going to Ethna

Road and his apartment. Then he showered and ran an electric shaver over his chin. He didn't try to get in touch with Claire until seven o'clock.

She sounded relieved to hear from him and asked him to visit.

'Do you think it's wise, honey?'

'Of course it is, Blake. I want to see you. Want to make sure that everything is all right.'

'I figure it is. I'll see you shortly.'

He drove into St Ann's Avenue with the mauve dusk steadily throttling the final shreds of daylight. The girl was waiting for him when he rang her doorbell. The door closed on them, she moved straight into his arms.

'Oh, Blake, I'm a bundle of nerves at the last moment,' she groaned. 'Do — do you think we should go through with it? I mean, there's nothing to prevent us calling it off, even at this late stage.'

'Are you crazy?' Denton cried. 'Nothing to prevent us calling it off? You're wrong, baby-face — utterly and completely wrong. There's twenty thousand bucks says we can't call it off. Do you realize I've already broken the law? I've been inside the joint after hours. Acting like a cat-burglar. I opened the front door, opened the door of Hank's hideyhole, opened his safe. It went like thin oil running through an engine. Sweet as a guy could wish it to be sweet.'

She shrugged, mustered a weak smile, and kissed him on the mouth.

'You're very brave, Blake.'

'You know nothing about me. I've got nerves of iron. Muscles of steel. Here, feel my biceps while I flex my arm.'

She laughed, kissing him again. Then she sobered.

'Why did Mr Otis switch Kirk for you today, Blake? I thought it a little strange.'

'Oh, hell, Claire. Stop putting bugs in the works, will you. Kirk was busy at important letters. Hank didn't want to disturb him. If you're going to hunt for dire significance in every trivial detail . . . '

'No, I'm not,' she said swiftly. 'Come into the kitchen and I'll fix some coffee. Have you eaten?'

He said he had. She seemed to marvel

at the cool way he said he had eaten. She said her stomach was so tense she couldn't coax it to take a bite of food.

'All I've been doing is drinking coffee.'

'What about a snort from the bottle? That should steady you.'

She didn't want to drink from the bottle. She advised him not to touch the bottle.

'I'm not going to touch it. All that jazz about fighters taking pep pills is over-rated. A healthy guy leaves his reflexes the way they are.'

While they drank coffee she asked him about the preparations he had made. He told her about the shovel and the rest of the paraphernalia in the trunk of his car. Her eyes glistened on his face as he talked.

'Where will you leave your car? You won't take it into Cable Street?'

'I'll leave the car at the corner of Felmoy Avenue. Otis likely left the money in the briefcase he brought from the bank.'

'He did,' she said, surprising him.

'You mean you were at the safe?'

'Yes. Just before we closed shop. You were at the washroom. I prepared some documents for Mr Otis and advised him to lock them in his safe. He told me to do it. The briefcase is in the safe all right.'

'Swell,' Denton said. 'All I have to do is snatch the briefcase, walk out into the night and get back to my car. Falling off a log couldn't be easier.'

'What time are you going to go there?'

'I'd reckoned on around two o'clock. By then the streets are quiet and Cable Street is like a morgue.'

'And afterwards?'

'I'll drive straight to Fosset's woods,' he said. 'It could be fatal to leave it until tomorrow. I'll find a spot to leave the dough. On the way back to town I'll get rid of the shovel. The cops might wonder what a guy living in an apartment wants with a shovel.'

'Get rid of the gloves as well. And when you return home make sure you clean your shoes, your trousers. You can't afford to leave a thing to chance, Blake.'

'I won't, he promised her. 'I've gone over each of the angles. I might have been a safe-breaker all my life for the way my brain is operating. I've got lots of potential, baby.'

'That just leaves tomorrow morning, when the robbery is discovered and the police are called in. We must face the fact that the police are going to suspect the staff at the outset.'

'I know. But we'll get through it, Claire.'

'Just one more thing, Blake,' she said slowly. 'Are you sure you don't want me to accompany you? I could stay in the car while you go to the office. Then there might be something I can do to help afterwards . . . '

'You must be nuts,' he said sharply. 'Bring you into it? I wouldn't hear of it. Now, drop that, will you.'

'I had to suggest it. It will ease my guilty conscience a little. You're doing most of the work.'

'A labour of love is what I call it, honey.'

★   ★   ★

He left the girl's apartment an hour later and drove back to Ethna Road. He cat-napped for a while, stirred, and settled down to watch a Western film on his portable TV. He found it impossible to concentrate. A vague thought was working at the fringes of his consciousness. When it hit him he sat up straight and stared at the wall.

The five-dollar bill on the floor. It really had been Claire's own money. She had put it there to test him. It had been a scrap of bait and he had grabbed it. She had had her eye on him since he started at *Advance*. She had seen him as a prospective partner in the crime he was going to pull off tonight. She was fed to the teeth with *Advance* and old Hank running hands over her. When she heard Hank was making another deal with Waterman she moved into action.

What did it mean, he asked himself. Really mean? That she was merely using him to help her get the money? That she would find some way of taking off on her own with the money and leave him in the lurch?

If that was her game she had another hunch coming. He would stash the suitcase in Fosset's woods and keep the exact location a secret until he could say with some degree of certainty which way the wind was blowing.

The more he thought of Claire Paige in this context the less he liked it. How could a woman be so devious and ruthless, a woman, moreover, whom he was sure he loved?

'It's wrong,' he told himself harshly. 'She wouldn't play such a dirty trick on me. But if she actually has a dirty trick on her mind . . . '

From there his thoughts shifted to the tall man again. He began growing moody, unsure of himself. He dug out a bottle of prime bourbon he had and swallowed three fingers from a glass. It was all negative thinking. He had had enough of negative thinking. The girl was on the level. She had proved she was on the level. Had she not offered to ride in the car with him tonight.

He tried to forget it.

By midnight he had recaptured most of

his former optimism. He would ring Claire and tell her about his fears. They would have a good laugh at them. No, he wouldn't ring her. He wouldn't let her suspect he distrusted her. It could spoil the swell symphony they had going.

He left his apartment at one-thirty. He drove without haste to the district where the warehouse was situated. He parked the Volkswagen at the corner of Felmoy and Cable street, got out and commenced walking. Cable Street was dim and quiet as before.

Denton strolled to the front of the warehouse building, fished the door key from his pocket and glanced about him before opening the door. He closed it gently behind him, switched on his flashlight and went along the fusty-smelling hall to reach the stairway.

At the bottom of the stairway he halted, raising his head to listen. It was only a car going past on the street. A tension had gripped him but it released his nerves and he began climbing. Nothing could go wrong with an easy number such as this. It was an easy number. No more dangerous than stealing pennies from a blind man's tin.

The weakened steps creaked but he let them creak. No one could hear the noise. The warehouse and the offices were empty. Even with twenty thousand in his safe upstairs, old Hank wouldn't dream of putting on a night guard. No one had ever broken into the building. No one ever would. It was the kind of place that offered no attraction for thieves.

He was in the big main office now, and he went forward with swift, deliberate steps to Hank's cubby-hole. You couldn't afford to get too smug. In this sort of action there were no medals given for foolhardiness. Get in there fast. Grab the loot. Get out fast. Get to Fosset's woods fast.

Hank's door was closed as before but it wasn't locked. It opened with that slight creak and Denton's flashlight touched the safe. The target. He stepped towards it, heard an odd, scratching noise behind him, and began to wheel in alarm.

He never made the complete turn. His senses went out in a loud explosion — as though a time-bomb had erupted under his skull.

His next awareness was of pain. It surged through his head in slow, agonizing reverberations. His mouth was dry and the walls of his throat appeared to have adhered together. There was a harsh, burning sensation at the backs of his eyes. He opened his eyes and coughed, fought to clutch at the drifting skirts of memory.

It came back like thunderheads rolling in on a vacuum created by lightning. Panic started in his loins and welled up through him. He was belly-flat on the dusty floor of Hank Otis' office. The flashlight had fallen from his hand when he fell and rolled under the office chair. The beam was focused on the panelled wall and a spider's web glistened like strands of silver.

Denton began to move and froze when realization hit him. The horror of it almost made him sick. Someone had been in Hank's office when he arrived. He had surprised whoever it was. That or the person had been waiting for him.

Who? Was he still here?

He wasn't here. Denton had the office to himself. Old Hank! Had Hank got the inspiration that someone would make a try for the tweny thousand? Had he decided to pay a late visit to ensure the money was intact? Then, when he heard the intruder, he had grabbed up a weapon and stood behind the door. He had slugged the intruder without bothering to ask questions or even challenge him.

Hell, yes, it could have happened that way. But where was Hank now — at this minute? Where but ringing in to police headquarters for the cops!

The panic in Denton threatened to overpower him, render his muscles and limbs flacid and stun his reflexes. He fought against the panic, sucked fetid air through his teeth and told himself to calm down.

So he was in a spot. All right. So he would have to get off it.

He moved, pushing himself to his knees. He would have to recover his flashlight. He would have to check the time. The time! He peered at the luminous face of his wrist watch. Ten after two. He couldn't have been out for long then, merely a matter of minutes. Relief swept over him. He could still make it. Behind Hank's office was a small doorway leading on to the fire escape. Good. That was how he would make his getaway.

His gloved hand touched a sticky substance on the floor and he caught his breath. What was this? Blood! Then he was bleeding. But no, he wasn't bleeding. There was no blood on his head, no blood on his face. Where the hell had the blood come from? It might not be blood. Ink. Or glue.

His eyes were growing accustomed to the gloom. He stood erect and had to grab the chair back to keep from falling. His head pounded as though a hammer were being slammed around in his skull. He took a step towards the flashlight. He seemed to stoop in slow motion to retrieve it.

His foot touched a yielding object and he could have screamed.

Oh, no. It couldn't be a body. It simply couldn't be a body. He hadn't hit anyone.

There hadn't been an opportunity to defend himself, never mind retaliate.

Clamping his jaws together in an iron vice, he snapped up the flashlight, then swung it to play on the object on the floor. It was a man. A man wearing a dark suit and a crisp, white shirt with bowtie. The shirt front had softened and gone gummy with blood. A bullet hole was there — a jagged indentation in the chest.

The flashlight shifted to the dead man's face and Denton's worst fears were realized. Hank Otis was dead, had been slain right here in his office.

Just then a coldness ran over Denton, not the paralysing chill of fear — although fear was there also in plenty — but a steadying coldness that throttled out his panic and allowed his brain to function normally and rapidly.

He went to the door and fumbled for the light switch. It triggered a glow that momentarily blinded him and sent raw pain surging in his skull. He blinked a few times and then took in the scene as a camera can capture a hundred details in a split second.

There was no doubt that Hank Otis was dead. He lay with his arms outstretched and one leg bent brokenly beneath his body. It was a contortion Hank couldn't have achieved when alive. His mouth and eyes were open, gaping emptily at the void he had been thrust into. Nearby him lay the snubnosed automatic which Denton had carried to and from the bank earlier in the day. The murder weapon for sure.

Next, Denton's gaze swept to the safe. The door stood open and when he went to look into it he saw only the documents and the cash box. The briefcase containing the twenty thousand dollars was gone.

Denton moved to the wall switch and snapped off the light. He realized that the killer might still be around. It was highly improbable, of course. The flashlight made a tiny, timid gleam in the darkness. He turned if off and started through the door to the outer office, his forehead slick with sweat.

His mind was racing at top speed now. The safe had been closed when he'd entered the office. It meant the killer hadn't opened it until he'd knocked him cold. But Hank Otis must have been dead by then. The body had been dragged to one side, then dragged back again. It hinted at a very cool customer having performed the deed.

Denton had gained the top of the stairway when the siren sounded. It rose as a tiny, cat-like wail and increased in volume as the police car or ambulance drew closer to Cable Street.

Once again panic fisted him in the solar-plexus and he gnashed his teeth in desperation. He started racing down the stairs, then halted and bounded back up them. If he went down to the street he would be caught in the jaws of a trap. But what was wrong with his thinking? He had intended leaving by the fire escape anyhow.

Should he leave? Should he run? Would it not be better to stay where he was till the cops arrived and then tell them the truth? Another query thudded sickeningly. Who had called the cops — Hank, before the killer got to him?

He didn't know. There were so many

loose ends here he couldn't even commence tying them up. But he mustn't stay. He must get off this hot spot immediately.

The sirens had wailed in to the front of the building. Others followed. Brakes caught and screeched protestingly. Doors slammed. Denton heard dim voices cracking orders.

He dashed through Hank Otis' office, to gain the door leading to the fire escape. The bolt was rusted home and sweat teemed down his jaws as he struggled with it. At last it rasped free and he thrust it back. He grabbed the door handle, hauled the door open. He stepped out to the catwalk hanging above the back alley, A cool breeze fanned his cheeks.

Feet were thumping into the alley on his right. Voices played back and forth. Cops' feet. Cops' voices.

Too late. He couldn't go down there. The only way he could go was up.

7

Denton went up.

He padded along the catwalk to the next flight of steps and began climbing them quickly. He prayed that the darkness was dense enough to shield his movements from the policemen in the alley below. But it wasn't. Glancing down, he could see their vague outlines, so that if they looked up they were bound to spot him.

What would they do if they did spot him — commence shooting? Ice water spilled over his spine. But why would they shoot at him? They wouldn't have had the time to investigate Hank Otis' office and find him dead. At this moment they were not looking for a killer, but merely for anything extraordinary.

How did he know what they were looking for, and how much they knew? One thing he was sure of — something had gone terribly wrong with the scheme he and Claire Paige had hatched. His immediate concern was to travel far away from this district with the utmost speed.

He was on a level with the roof of the warehouse building and he stepped gingerly on to it. He went off balance fractionally and almost fell backwards. His heart skipped a beat and then began hammering against his ribs.

A voice rasped up from the alley below. 'There's a guy on the roof . . . '

'Hey, there. Hold it!'

Denton tore across the roof, ducking a chimney stack, hitting a sudden black slope that sent him tumbling downwards, sliding and clawing. He reached the bottom and sprang up, dazed and shaken. There was another slope in front of him and he went up it on all fours. He reached a brick wall and paused briefly, panting for breath, staring at a black maw beneath him. It was the lowest point in the pitch of a roof of a different building.

He let go and dropped.

He landed fairly well, lunged erect, and ran across a flat roof. It finished at the base of a high wall which he couldn't possibly climb. He swore in frustration. Sweat was streaming from his forehead and his heart threatened to burst free of his rib-cage.

He hunted about him like an animal at bay. He came on a rusted iron railing and gripped it. It proved to be an iron ladder and Denton scrambled up it. It was all of twelve feet high and made him a perfect target from the alley below. Nobody shouted. It meant they had left the alley and were searching for means to get up on to the roofs.

There was no ladder on the other side, but the roof here was elevated and a four-foot drop put him down on it. It was a flat roof and he sped over it, ducking chimney stacks, striving to find firm purchase for his feet without slackening his stride.

He must have travelled a hundred yards from the warehouse building when he heard a yell behind him.

'I see him. I see him!'

'Stand where you are, mister!'

The cops had reached the high wall and were perched there. Something whined past Denton's head a split second before he heard the flat, vicious crack of a revolver.

They were shooting at him! They were trying to bring him down. Fear clawed at Denton with the realization he would be shot if he didn't halt to surrender.

Surrender. Why should he surrender? He hadn't murdered Hank Otis. He wasn't going to be a fall guy for the real killer. Why the hell didn't the cops concentrate on the killer and leave him alone?

Five minutes later he was on yet another flat roof. Beyond, he could see street lights glowing in the distance. The sound of an occasional automobile driving past drifted to his ears.

He halted suddenly when he saw a glow of light off on his left. The light was on the roof and seemed to be escaping from a hole or window. A skylight! In desperation he scurried towards it. His legs were weak with all the climbing and running he had put in. His lungs appeared to be on fire.

The skylight was open about six inches.

It measured about two feet square. He kneeled and gazed into a room beneath him. He saw an artist's easel with a strong lamp focused on a half-finished painting. It was a painting or a drawing. He thought he saw a moving shadow. Yes, there it was. A woman. He could see her dark hair. Dare he take a chance? He must take a chance.

He rattled on the glass with his fingers.

She came and looked up at him. Her face was pale and the eyes that stared at him wide with alarm.

'Please let me in.'

'Who are you? What are you doing here?'

'Let me in,' he pleaded. 'I won't hurt you. I promise that I won't.'

She continued staring at him for what seemed an age, trying to make up her mind. Away off on the roofs Denton heard the scratching and scrambling of feet. There was a heavy clattering and someone cursed.

'It's too high,' the woman below Denton was saying. 'Try and open it yourself.'

He did so, putting himself at full length and stretching his hand along the transom. Try as he did he couldn't reach the bar governing the distance the skylight could be opened. The slithering feet were drawing closer. Fear gathered in his stomach and he felt sick and giddy.

'If you stood on a chair . . . '

'I'll try.'

She moved from his vision and he thought she would never return. Then he saw a chair being placed directly below him. A moment later she was standing on it and releasing the holding bar. Denton had his fingers clutching the frame in case she meant to close him out. Their eyes met.

'Pull it open,' she said.

He did so. She was calmer than many women would have been. She looked like someone who had been around and who knew her way around. Denton swung the frame right back on its hinges, letting it rest on the roof.

'Get off the chair and I'll drop.'

'But — '

'Snap it up,' he barked, hearing an

exchange of voices off on the next roof.

'Did he come this way?'

'Sure he did. The bastard. Why couldn't he stand.'

'He'll stand when he catches a slug in his fanny.'

Denton wriggled his body into the opening, speaking to the woman as he did so.

'Kill the light.'

'Are you crazy?'

'Do as you're told, damn it.'

He poised and grabbed the edge of the skylight frame, drawing it towards him. He lowered his body gradually until he was able to take the weight of the skylight on the crown of his head.

As he dropped the room was plunged into darkness. The skylight made a noisy snapping sound as it fell home. Denton hit the floor and hunched there, looking for the woman in the shadows. He made out her form by the door where the light switch was located.

'Don't move,' he entreated. 'Don't scream. I'm not going to hurt you.'

She didn't say anything. Her eyes

glowed in the dark.

He peered up at the skylight now, hearing the dim scraping of feet. The movements ceased and there was silence. Then he heard measured voices.

'I figured I saw a light.'

'From the street. From here some-where ... Hey, a skylight! Do you suppose ...'

The cop was on his knees on the roof, trying to look down into the room. His face and shoulders blotted out the feeble glow of starshine. Denton held his breath, forgetting the woman by the door. His shirt was clinging to his back. His calf and thigh muscles ached.

A muted creak warned him.

'Don't open it,' he said in a savage whisper.

There was another creak, but she hadn't opened the door. The shadow was removed from the glass above him. The voices again.

'Do you want to go in there?'

'Come on. We'll head for the street. Mind you don't step into space.'

Feet scraped, went into motion, receded.

The sounds died and left only silence again.

'Can I switch on the light?'

'Wait a few minutes,' he said, adding quickly, 'Please.'

'Whatever you say. They're police, aren't they?'

'Yes, I think so.'

'You don't know?' She sounded surprised. 'I heard sirens a short time ago.'

'Yeah, they are cops,' he said gruffly. 'But they're not after me.'

'Oh . . . '

He laughed mirthlessly.

'That makes me nuts? But I'm not nuts, lady. Look . . . are you here on your own?'

She didn't answer that. Likely she thought it would be wiser not to. He could be a dangerous maniac for all she knew about him. She certainly had a lot of nerve. Another dame would have screamed to high heaven. He ought to be grateful to her. He was grateful to her, extremely grateful. She had saved his skin, given him protection. For how long would she be willing to protect him?

'It doesn't matter,' he went on gently. 'I mean, whether you're on your own. But don't make a fuss, huh?'

The light went on suddenly and he started in alarm, staring at her. She was tall and slim, dark-haired and dark-eyed. She was wearing some kind of smock that had paint daubed over it. There was a capable, competent air about her. Her eyes were running from his head to his feet, from his feet to his head; they settled on his face.

'Relax,' she said. 'I'm not going to scream. Unless you have ideas about getting violent.'

He smiled meagrely.

'No, I'm not going to get violent. I'm not a violent man.'

'I heard sirens,' she said. 'It was the police. They were after you?'

'No, I mean yes! Oh, hell. I'm not sure what I mean. But don't panic,' he added swiftly. 'I'm not a nut either. I just happened to wander into a situation that turned out to be explosive. The cops must be after someone else. I lost my head when they spotted me and took to the roofs.'

Her expression said it was a plausible story, but it didn't hold much water for her. Still, she wasn't frightened of him and that was something. She appeared to have weighed him up in her mind and concluded she could handle him.

He made a gesture to the easel. There was a half-finished painting there of a girl in a swimsuit. She was standing on a stretch of sand and seemed to be gazing out to sea.

'All your own work?'

'That's right,' she said in a non-committal voice. 'It was progressing nicely until you dropped in.'

'I'm sorry. Do you usually work this late?'

'Not usually. When the spirit moves me. Tonight it moved me.'

He was gazing around him at the clutter of paintings and canvasses when she opened the room door.

'Where are you going?' Denton snapped.

'Into the living room. Come on. Could you do with a cup of coffee?'

'Yes, I could.' His tone was suspicious.

He had no idea whether she lived alone. She might be married for all he knew. Or she could have a man living with her even if she wasn't married. 'Are you on your own?'

She walked out of the room and he hurried after her, switching off the light before he left. He realized he was still wearing the rubber gloves and that the girl would have noticed. He peeled them off and pushed them into his jacket pocket with the flashlight. He had scraped his knee on one of the walls and it pained him a little.

He finished up in a small but comfortably-furnished living room where there were three easy chairs, a large couch, and a television set on a stand. A lot of magazines were lying around. She made a motion at the chairs.

'Have a seat. I'll fix the coffee.'

There was a dinette with a kitchen area at the rear. She went from his sight and Denton went after her. She turned to gaze questioningly at him. She shrugged and went to the gas stove. She was about twenty-five or so, he guessed. She was attractive in a hard, polished fashion. Her dark hair was done up in a beehive style, leaving the slim, white column of her neck bare.

'There isn't much room for two in here.'

'We'll manage if we crush together,' he said wryly.

'You don't trust me, do you?'

'Of course I trust you.'

'Well, I don't trust you, big fellow. So don't get too close, will you.'

He perched on a stool and brought out his cigarettes. He offered her one but she shook her head. He lit his cigarette and puffed hungrily. Already the tension was easing out of him. But he'd better not allow his guard to drop too far. Those cops were on the loose. They would go on searching. They might come rapping at the door anytime. He watched the girl make the coffee.

'What is your name?'

'What is it to you?' she said carelessly.

'Okay. If that's how you want it.' He went on smoking.

'What is yours?'

'I — uh — Look, drop it, will you.'

'It's all the same to me. My name is Olive Overton. I'm trying to make a living as a commercial artist. I do stuff for advertising outfits, magazines occasionally.'

'You must have a ball.'

'At three o'clock in the morning? Be reasonable, mister. It's a difficult grind. It's a hard old world.'

'Oh, I've noticed,' he said, grinning faintly. 'I've noticed.'

'Do you like being a burglar?'

'Hey, hold on. I'm not a burglar.'

'Sorry. My mistake. So you're some kind of a surgeon that has to chase his patients over the rooftops?'

'The rubber gloves? Yeah, I know. It must look highly suspicious.'

'Only if you've got a suspicious mind.'

'I'm not a burglar. Not really. I had something on tonight. A mission you could call it . . . '

'Sure. Then you're a spy. CIA. I'll buy it if you want me to. But those were police?'

'Yeah, they were.' He sighed, puffing at

his cigarette, trying to channel his thoughts into the direction they should be taking. Hank Otis dead. Murdered. The cops chasing him. The cops could find him here. Could pin a murder label on his jacket. He would have to get word to Claire Paige, let her know what had taken place.

'You've got a phone out there. Could I use it?'

'Help yourself. Are you going to turn yourself in? If you've done nothing too silly, you ought to.'

'I have done something silly.'

He left her and went back to the living room. He sat down by the wall niche where the telephone was located. He lifted the receiver and began to dial. He had dialled two digits when he changed his mind and replaced the instrument on its hook.

'Coffee's ready.'

She had come into the living room behind him, carrying a tray. She laid the tray on a coffee table and Denton went over to it.

'Thanks, Olive. I could use this.'

'But not the phone? Have you taken cold feet?'

'I wasn't going to call the cops.'

'I didn't think you were. Your confederate? Your girl, maybe?'

'You're a very sharp kid.'

'Very, very sharp.'

She didn't smile when she said that. Denton lifted a cup of black coffee and took it to a chair. He was drinking thirstily when the doorbell buzzed. He almost dropped the coffee.

'Who's that?' he demanded hoarsely.

'Why ask me? I'm not expecting anybody. You are, mister. The police.'

Sweat made a gummy paste on Denton's brow. He rose and placed the cup back on its tray. The girl was staring off to the front of the apartment. Her expression told him nothing.

'Don't answer it,' he pleaded.

'Take it easy. If I don't answer they might beat the door down.' She pointed. 'My bedroom is through there. Bring your coffee with you just in case.'

He hesitated momentarily, reluctant to leave his fate in the girl's hands. She didn't wait to see his reaction. She began walking out of the living room to gain the front door.

Denton lifted the coffee cup again and headed for the bedroom. As he reached it the buzzer commenced ringing afresh and went on ringing.

8

The girl opened the apartment door.

'Yes?' Denton heard her saying. 'What is it?'

'Sorry to disturb you, lady. We're police officers. An office was broken into along the street. A man was spotted on the run across the roofs a short time ago. We're trying to find him. Your apartment has a skylight, does it not?'

'Yes, it does . . . '

'This is the place, Sarge. Greg and me figured we saw the guy in the vicinity of this roof. We saw a light, but the light went out. Then we found the skylight, and — '

'Now look,' the girl called Olive Overton interrupted crisply, 'I've been working late. Now I'm finished. I'm tired and I want to get to bed. If you would be so kind as to say exactly what you want with me . . . '

'We'd like to search your apartment, Miss — '

'Overton. Olive Overton. I'm sorry,' she went on in the same cool manner. 'You cannot search my apartment.'

'But why not, lady?' the sergeant said.

'Because I say so,' she snapped.

'We could get a warrant, lady,' the officer told her.

'Lay off, Fisher,' the sergeant admonished. 'Let me do the talking.' His voice softened to a tone he likely thought was more reasonable, and less objectionable to the girl. 'All right, Miss Overton. We don't want to put you about. But you do understand we want to catch this guy.'

'Of course.'

'Then maybe you wouldn't mind answering a couple of questions.'

'If they are not lengthy questions, Officer. As I said, I'm tired and wish to get to bed.'

'Sure, sure. You've been working late, you said. Does it mean you work out someplace — in a club or something of that nature? You've just returned home?'

Olive Overton laughed thinly. There was no amusement in her laugh.

'You seem to have got it wrong. I don't

go out anywhere to work. Not often anyhow. I certainly wasn't out tonight. I'm a commericial artist. Free-lance. I work right here at home.'

'Oh! Then you haven't been out, lady?'

'I told you. I haven't been out. Nobody has come in through my skylight,' she added with another thin laugh. 'Had anyone dared to, your department would have heard of it before now.'

'Looks like a bum steer, Sarge,' the officer grumbled.

'Yeah. Well, I — Did you check the skylight recently, Miss? Do you keep it open through the day?'

'Usually I do. I stand on a chair to open it. At night, when I finish work in my studio, I close it.'

'You had a light burning in there?' the officer asked

'Yes, I had. I switched it off.'

'When?' the sergeant said.

'Ten minutes ago. Fifteen. Listen, if you really must see for yourself, you'd better come and look.'

'Good idea, lady.'

In the bedroom, Denton froze when he

heard the heavy feet crossing the hall to the living room. If that fox-brained officer strode to this door and opened it he would be lost. The girl too. She was going out on a limb to help him. He wondered why. He didn't know why. He didn't care why.

They were talking in the studio.

'You can see there is nothing in here,' the girl was saying in her cool, unruffled manner. 'Satisfied?'

A pause. Then, 'There's dirt here on the floor, Sarge. Right beneath the skylight.'

'Well, I'll be! So there is . . . How about it, Miss Overton? It's dirt from the roof, I'm sure — '

'It's paint,' the girl broke in quickly. 'Hardened paint. I make a mess. I was scraping a spatula.'

'A what?'

'This thing here. You can see the dark paint. It gets hard when it sits for too long. I was too tired to clean up properly.'

Listening to them, sweat streamed down Denton's forehead and jaws. He was tensed to the limit. Everything depended on the cops believing what the girl said. Footsteps were moving from the studio again. The sergeant was talking. His voice was a good deal deeper than the harness man's.

'Sorry we had to bust in on you, lady. But we have to keep trying.'

'I understand. I hope you catch the man.'

'Oh, we'll catch him. Say, I didn't know there was a residential block in this street.'

'There are a few attic apartments,' the girl explained to him. 'They come cheaper than the conventional apartment.'

'If you can put up with the racket going on throughout the day, huh?'

'You get used to it,' the girl said.

'I guess so.' They were in the hallway once more, heading for the outer door. Denton began to relax. They halted before opening the door. 'By the way, lady, I'd keep that skylight secured until morning if I were you. And if you happen to hear or notice anything odd, you'll ring in?'

'Yes, I will, of course.'

The door opened.

'One more thing, Officer. What is the man you are after supposed to have done?'

What the hell, Denton thought grimly in the darkness of the bedroom. So she didn't trust him too far at all. He waited in suspense to hear the sergeant's response.

'He's a killer, lady. He murdered a man who runs a mail order set-up along the street. Well . . . thanks again. Sorry to have barged in on you.'

The girl did not answer him. The door closed. Silence. Denton's jaws clamped together so tightly they hurt. His heart was hammering like a steam-driven piston. He moved out of the room slowly, crossed to the living room. The girl was standing in the doorway, her face whiter than ever, her eyes dark and wide, and luminous with anxiety. She noticed him and stared.

'Don't look at me like that. The cop is wrong. He's all mixed up. I didn't kill him.'

'You're lying, aren't you?'

'No, I'm not lying. Damn it, no! I'm not lying.' His voice had risen and she backed to the doorway. He saw fright in her gaze now, real fright. She had been willing to help a lame duck off a spot, but she had no intention of helping a killer. Why had she not told the cops then? Why didn't she grab her opportunity when it was within easy reach? Did it mean she doubted he was a killer, that she was prepared to let him have the benefit of her doubts?

'I'm going to go and tell them,' she said and made a dash for the front door.

He went after her and clutched her shouders. His fingers dug into the soft flesh and she winced painfully.

'You're hurting me.'

'I don't want to hurt you. I won't hurt you. I couldn't hurt you in a hundred years of trying. But please listen to me, will you.'

'Let me go,' she demanded.

'You promise you won't run?'

'I'm not going to run.'

He released her. He held her elbow

gently and brought her back into the living room. He felt an involuntary shudder race through her.

'Please sit down,' he said.

She took one of the easy chairs and he brought out his cigarettes. The pack was crumpled and the cigarettes were mashed. He extracted two, straightened them and offered her one.

'Go on, you could do with a smoke.'

She accepted the cigarette wordlessly and placed it between her lips. He flicked his lighter for her and then for himself. He stood looking down at the girl.

'I realize it must seem bad to you,' he began slowly. 'I know it would seem bad to anyone in the same situation. But it's all wrong. I didn't kill him.'

The dark eyes lifted to his own, clashed squarely and held fixedly.

'You know who he is?'

'The dead man? Sure, I know. He's my boss. One of my bosses. His name is Hank Otis.' He waited to see if she had heard of Hank Otis, but she hadn't. The name meant nothing to her. Denton sighed and continued. 'He and Jack

Rhodes run the *Advance Mail Order* company between them. It happened this way — oh, hell . . . I don't know where to begin. I don't know if you'll believe a single word I say.'

'Start at the beginning,' she said.

'You really want to hear? You wouldn't prefer that I head out of here and left you to call back the cops?'

She took a drag on the cigarette. She wasn't used to smoking and she coughed a bit.

'Please yourself,' she said. 'Run if you must. There's nothing much I can do to stop you.'

'But you'd ring in to the cops when I'd gone?'

'I guess I would. Wouldn't you if you were in my shoes?'

'I guess I would.' He mopped his forehead and jaws with a handkerchief. His legs were beginning to feel weak under him and he dragged over one of the other chairs and sank down on it. 'Okay then, Olive. Pin your ears back and listen to my story. But it isn't going to make the best reading.'

'You still haven't told me your name.'

'I'll tell you now. My name is Blake Denton. I'm employed as a typist with *Advance* . . . '

He was to wonder later why he told the girl everything. He could easily have walked out of the apartment and carried on running. But maybe he had run far enough, and the idea of becoming a fugitive was the least attractive one he had at that moment.

He talked and went on talking, describing how Claire had told him of the twenty thousand dollars that would be lodged overnight in Hank Otis' safe, and how he and Claire meant to get their hands on the money. He explained in detail his arrival at the warehouse, his being slugged on the head as he stepped into Hank's private office.

'I couldn't have been out for long. Only minutes at the most. It was like having walked into a nightmare. There was Hank Otis on the floor — shot dead with his own gun. There was the open safe. It had been rifled by the killer and the briefcase containing the twenty grand had vanished.

'I was trying to gather my wits when I heard the sirens coming into the street. I was so confused I started down although I'd planned on leaving by the fire escape route. I pulled myself together, got out through the escape door, and made it on to the roof. I nearly fell. There were cops pouring into the alley and they spotted me. I took off over the roofs. The cops came after me. One of them took a shot at me. I figured I was a gone goose when I saw the glow coming from the skylight. I went to it like a moth going to a candle, and here I am.'

She said nothing when he had finished. She just sat there with the forgotten cigarette between her fingers and stared at him. There was a quality in her gaze that set up a prickling sensation at the nape of Denton's neck.

Finally he could stand her silence no longer.

'You don't believe a word, huh?'

'What does it matter whether or not I believe you?' she countered in her crisp, controlled voice.

132

'It matters a hell of a lot to me,' he retorted. 'You dragged me out of a hole, didn't you? You're entitled to an explanation. I've given you an explanation. I don't want you to think I'm a killer, honey. Don't you see? I'm not a killer. A potential thief, yes. I saw a tasty slice of bait dangling in front of my nose and I grabbed it. I was a fool. Okay, I was a fool. But I'm not a killer. I didn't murder Hank Otis. Somebody else did. Somebody beat me to it tonight, got in there in front of me, murdered Hank and took off with the dough.'

'Who else knew it would be there?'

'I — ' Denton stopped speaking, gaping at her. He went on thickly, 'What are you trying to prove, Olive?'

She shrugged. She laid the half-smoked cigarette on a saucer. She rose and went across the living room.

'Where are you going?'

'To make more coffee.'

He followed her into the kitchen. His head throbbed. His legs ached. There was a pain in the middle of his back that he hadn't felt before. This was like an extension of the nightmare. Meeting this girl, confessing everything to her. What had made him do it? Why was he so anxious to have her believe him? He was a fool. Of course he was a fool. Immediately he left her she would get on with the cops and tell them all he had told her.

Another thought hit him like a thunderbolt.

'Don't bother making coffee for me, Olive. I've got to get out of here. I've got to make it back to my place before the police go there. The first thing they'll do on failing to catch the killer is make the rounds of the *Advance* employees. It might be daylight before they get to my place, but it might not. It's possible they'll start off with the people who worked directly under Hank.'

She laid the coffee pot down and turned to him. She was capable of drawing on a blank expression that was a wall against her thoughts. He had no way of knowing what was passing through her mind.

'How did you reach Cable Street?'

'I came by car. My own car. It's a

Volkswagen. I left it parked at the corner of Felmoy Avenue and Cable.'

'Where do you live?'

He told her. She eyed him steadily, mulling it all over.

'They'd catch you before you reached your car,' she stated.

'I've got to try, Olive. I've got to do it fast, too. I can sneak out and start walking. I can reach Felmoy by a roundabout route.'

He was striding to the door when she called after him. 'Wait, Blake. I may be able to help you . . . '

'How?' he said, swinging as she came towards him. 'You would go and collect my car? You must be crazy. If the cops stopped you they would recognize you. Do you really want to stick your neck out that far?'

'I've got a car. It's in a basement garage.'

'The basement of this building?' He frowned at her, wondering if she was planning a sell-out after all, but on a more elaborate scale than he'd envisaged.

'Yes. I could go down and get it. By this

time the police will have moved away from the area, extending the scope of their search. And they might have caught the killer,' she added. 'The real killer.'

He eyed her warily. He shook his head.

'The real killer was too slick, honey. He had everything planned too well to leave room for a loophole.'

'You can't imagine how the police received the alarm?'

'I haven't got a clue, except one that says the killer tried to rope me in as a fall guy. Listen,' he went on, 'even if you took me home in your car I'd still have to collect my own car.'

She shrugged her shoulders.

'Suit yourself. Perhaps your girl-friend might have a better idea if you got in touch with her. You were going to ring her, weren't you? You changed your mind. Don't you think you can trust her?'

Denton didn't answer that one. He thought swiftly. One thing stuck out a mile. He would have to get back to his place with all possible speed. If he didn't and the police visited, he would be sunk without an alibi.

'All right, Olive. You're a sport. We'll try it your way, but with a variation. If you can get me into Felmoy Avenue somehow without us being spotted, I'll pick up my own car and use it to drive myself home.'

'Stay here until I return.'

She pulled off the paint-daubed smock, revealing a short-skirted blue dress beneath it. Without glancing at him she left the apartment.

Denton stood on in the living room and lit another cigarette. She was taking him for a stupe, he told himself. She was as frightened as hell in case he murdered her also. She had fed him that yarn in order to make a painless escape from him. Once down in the street she would make for the first phone booth and tell the police where he was.

Panic seized him. He fought against it. The dame had had ample opportunity to turn him in and she had let it slip. It meant she didn't take him for a killer. Just by looking at him she knew he wasn't a killer.

'Big deal!' he grunted sourly. But he had placed his trust in her, and even if he was tempted to make a run for it now he wouldn't get far.

She was back in five minutes. Her features were tense and her eyes glowed.

'The street is quiet,' she told him. 'There are a lot of cars parked a couple of hundred yards away but they won't notice us drive off.'

'You just hope, honey. That foxey cop could be staked out on the other side of the road. But let's go. I can't afford to stay here any longer.'

She took him down in a service elevator, and when they hit the dark thoroughfare she told him to wait until she got behind the wheel of her convertible. Then she signalled, holding the off-side door open for him. Denton dashed to the car and seated himself. The car moved from the curb, heading for the end of the street and away from the vehicles crowding the front of the *Advance Mail Order* building.

9

The girl was a cool and capable driver.

She took Denton away from Cable Street, through a maze of side streets and back alleys, and then, seven short minutes later, she slid along Felmoy Avenue and halted at the rear of the Volkswagen.

'That's your car?'

'That's it.' He pierced the shadows before reaching for the door. 'It's nothing short of miraculous. I've made it, and there isn't a cop in sight.'

'You haven't made it home yet,' she said tonelessly. 'You'd better check to make sure your car's okay.'

He glanced sharply at her. 'I'd better.' He slid to the road and went to the Volkswagen, using his keys to open the driving side door. Behind the wheel he gunned the engine. If she'd expected his car to be somehow immobilized she was wrong.

He stuck his head out as the convertible's motor revved. The car went into a tight U-turn and set off along the avenue, going back the way they had come.

She hadn't even waited to say so-long or good luck. Denton shrugged. It was possible she had taken fright at the last moment. He didn't think so, though. She was much to cool and collected to frighten easily.

He didn't stay to work it out.

He imitated the girl's U-turn to avoid having to enter Cable Street. He drove at a reasonable speed until he was clear of Felmoy Avenue. Then he jammed his shoe down on the gas pedal.

He was approaching Ethna Road when a thought hit him. It brought him out in another cold sweat. The shovel, suitcase, and sheet of plastic in the trunk! If the cops were waiting at his apartment building and decided to make a search of the car — as they undoubtedly would — how would he explain the items, the shovel in particular?

Stifling a curse, he drove away from his street, veering to the suburbs where he found a plot of waste ground flanked by a hedge. He stopped the car and looked about him to make sure the coast was clear. It was, and he flung the shovel and the sheet of plastic over the hedge. He remembered the spare pair of rubber gloves, dug these out also and pitched them into the darkness. He had another pair of gloves in his pocket! He whipped them free and got rid of them. Just then he really felt like a killer who had to get rid of incriminating evidence.

The suitcase he couldn't throw away, as there was the possibility of it being traced back to him.

His shirt clinging coldly to his back, he slumped behind the wheel, slammed the door. Still another thought surfaced in his mind. The duplicate key he had made . . .

'What a stupid punk I am. If the cops picked me up with a key to the warehouse I'd be sunk.'

He fished it out and sent it spinning into the shadows.

Driving away from the spot, doubts began to gnaw at him. He had acted too rashly there. He should have taken more time to figure the moves. If someone discovered that stuff they might get in touch with the cops. The cops were liable to put two and two together and link the stuff with the killing of Hank Otis. All they had to do was try the key in the front door of the warehouse and their theory would be proved. And he had handled everything with his bare hands!

Denton was tempted to return and retrieve the items. But he was fighting against time, and it was more important that he reach his apartment before a squad of police officers got there. He carried on driving.

Ethna Road looked quiet and deserted as he eased into it and cruised to the front of his apartment building. He left his car in its customary niche and sat for several seconds looking around him. No police cars. No waiting men. No action of any kind. His heart took an upward swing. It might be okay. He might have extricated himself from the whole horrible situation in the nick of time.

He alighted and locked the Volkswagen. He went into the dimly-lit lobby and it was empty also. He climbed the stairway to his apartment on the third floor. In the passage he felt bushed, thoroughly deflated. The adrenalin was dying in him and he felt weak and beaten.

He let himself into his apartment with the minimum of noise, closed and locked the door behind him and made for the cupboard where he kept a bottle of scotch. With two rapid shots beneath his belt he began to relax. His brain persisted in operating at full stretch. Claire. He would have to contact her immediately and explain what had happened. She would be expecting to hear from him, in any case. Apart from all that, it could be disastrous if the police got to her before he did.

First things first, though. The police could come to him before they went to Claire. Or they could plan simultaneous visits to prevent them exchanging notes. He wondered if the cops had been here already. He didn't think they had. If they had zoomed in on his apartment and seen he wasn't at home, they would have left a look-out to keep tabs on him.

Before ringing Claire's place he stripped and put on pyjamas. Then he took his jacket, pants and shoes to the bathroom and gave them a thorough brushing over the tub, paying particular attention to the soles of his shoes. Satisfied, he ran enough water to carry the dust and dirt away. A few minutes later he sat down at the phone and dialled Claire's number.

It was a long time before she answered.

The sound of her voice, when it came, startled him.

'Is it you, Blake?' She sounded as though she were surprised to hear from him. There was a distinct quaver in her tone. But why not? She must have been sitting on a basket of eggs since he spoke with her last.

'Of course it's me, honey. Look,' he went on swiftly, 'I don't want to say too much over the phone. But get yourself prepared for a visit from the cops.'

'What!' Her voice had soared and taken on an edge of panic. 'But why, Blake? Did something go wrong? Yes, something did go wrong, didn't it?

144

'Too true it did. I — I don't want to relate the whole story over the phone. Just pay attention to me. If the police call, try and behave normally. You don't know a thing. You are shocked and grieved at the news they bring you. Right?'

'What news, Blake? What are you saying? Surely you didn't make a mess of it . . . '

'I didn't make the mess, baby. Somebody else did. Listen, all you have to do is react normally. Forget that we ever got together in the first place. But get one point fixed firmly and permanently in your brain, Claire. I didn't do it.'

'Do what?' she cried angrily.

He bit his lip in chagrin, knowing that he ought to give her the entire story, but fearful of committing himself. Still, he would have to give her enough to put her curiosity at rest.

'You know H,' he said tautly.

'Have you gone crazy, Blake? But yes — I think I know what you mean. H. O.?'

'That's right, baby. He was there. Somebody else was there too. They got to him first. Then they got at me. I slipped out in the nick of time.'

'Blake — ' Her voice was a thin, frightened scrape of sound. ' — are you saying he is — '

'Yeah, I am. Now just forget it. You've got to be able to react as though you're completely in the dark. I'll see you as soon as possible, and tell you everything.'

'Yes. All — all right, Blake . . . '

He held the receiver to his ear for another moment, not speaking, listening until she hung up. He replaced the instrument on its hook, lit a cigarette, and sat staring off into space.

He wondered how long it would be before the cops arrived.

★ ★ ★

Denton glanced at his wristwatch. It was four-thirty in the morning. He couldn't understand it. The police should have been here long ago. What was keeping them? Had they really been to his apartment earlier — before he managed to reach home — just checked that he wasn't there, and gone away again? He

146

didn't have the answer. What he did have was a hundred niggling doubts and fears.

He had not moved from the chair beside the telephone. He had sat there, smoking, until there was nothing left to smoke, and his mouth was dry and sour-tasting, and his tongue resembled a piece of rotted rope.

He had been going over every angle of the incident in an effort to get to the bottom of the mystery. It was nothing less than a mystery. What had drawn Hank Otis to his office where the money was stashed? What had drawn the killer? Who had rung in the alarm to the police? What had been the precise content of that alarm?

Next he had thought of the girl, Olive Overton, tried to cope with the questions stemming from his contact with her. Why had she helped him and not turned him in? Had she helped him in order to lull him into a sense of security, knowing there would be lots of time afterwards to get the police and tell them the tale? If she had done that and gone to the cops, why hadn't the cops come here to get him before now? Again, what had possessed him to make a clean breast to the girl? He had told her his story as though she had been a bosom companion since kindergarten days. It was amazing. There were depths and nooks and corners to his personality that he hadn't been aware existed.

He must have dozed for a while.

When he awoke it was ten after five and daylight had come to the air. He was slumped on the chair with his head on his chest and he roused, yawned sleepily and stared at his watch again. The cops were not coming after all. He ought to get into bed and have a couple of hours' proper sleep.

He knew he wouldn't sleep. Immediately he stirred, his brain had commenced clicking into action. It would give him no rest.

He went to the kitchenette and fixed a pot of coffee. He considered calling Claire again and asking if the police had been to her. He decided against this. If he rang and the cops were at her apartment, one of them might answer the phone and their collusion would be out. Even if he hung up on hearing a strange voice from Claire's end, the damage would be done and they would smell a rat. Better to wait, be patient, and meet the day as it came.

By eight he was washed, shaved and dressed, and faced with the prospect of having to set off to *Advance* to commence his day's work as usual. But of course there would be no work today. The warehouse and offices would be closed and under the charge of the police. Everyone would be standing around with stunned features, discussing the murder and trying to figure out who would have done for old Hank.

Just then Denton wondered if he shouldn't set off early and call with Olive Overton. It would give him the chance of checking out the girl's reactions this morning and whether she had gone to the police.

No, he wouldn't do that. If the girl had gone to the police they would have her apartment under surveillance. Believing him to be a killer, they may expect him to go after her with the intention of killing her also, to ensure that she wouldn't talk.

At eight-thirty Denton set out for Cable Street.

Half-way to his destination he had an idea and stopped off at a newsstand to buy the local paper. Back in the Volkswagen, he scanned through it from the front page to the back one. Then he frowned and dug his teeth into his underlip. No mention of the slaying of Hank Otis! What did it mean? What the hell *could* it mean?

It meant one thing only. The cops were playing it close to the chest. They thought they had the solution in the bag and didn't want their pitch fouled up with premature publicity.

Denton didn't like it. He would have preferred a blaze of publicity and an account of last night's roof-top chase in Cable Street. The account might have given him a pointer as to his best plan of behaviour. It was useless thinking the killing had happened too late to make the morning edition. The morning edition would stay open until three or three-thirty, at least.

He balled the newspaper and stuffed it into the glove compartment. He began driving again. There was a block of ice where his spine should be, and his nerve centre seemed to be infested by a million restless bugs.

He had another shock when he reached Cable Street and the building where *Advance* was located. There wasn't a police car in sight. Nor a police officer. The cars owned by the staff were on the parking area. He saw Claire's car and parked the Volkswagen next to it. He was a few minutes later than his usual time of arrival in the mornings. That had been due to his stopping at the newsstand and then going through the *Maxwell Herald*.

A possible explanation for the atmosphere of normality occurred to him. The cops could be playing it smart. They had urged Jack Rhodes to open up the warehouse and say nothing of the killing. They were hoping that one of the employees would fail to appear for work this morning, leaving them with their number one suspect.

The notion put a chill in Denton's

blood. Okay then. If that was the game, he would go along with it to the limit.

He entered the hallway, climbed the stairs to the dispatch office, and went inside. A glance showed him Claire Paige at her desk, and Sally Baines at her desk. There was no sign of Kirk Mason.

Sally looked round and bade him a cheery good morning.

'Hi, Sally,' he said from a constricted throat. 'Good morning, Miss Paige.'

He saw Claire's shoulders stiffen before she turned slightly to look at him. Her flat expression told him absolutely nothing.

'Good morning, Denton' Her tone was neutral.

He went to his own desk in a sort of a trance. The whole setup was screwy, crazy as a nightmare. And maybe it had been nothing worse than a nightmare after all. He had dreamed the sock on the head, Hank Otis' dead body, the nerve-racking chase across the roof-tops, Olive Overton's attic apartment.

He had work hanging over from the previous day and he started on it, his hands hovering above the typewriter automatically, as though they weren't his at all, but someone else's hands.

After a few minutes his gaze shifted to the door of Hank Otis' cubby-hole. At any second now old Hank would emerge and cross to Claire's desk. Denton had a wild urge to laugh hysterically. Somehow he controlled himself.

Where was Kirk Mason? Where was Jack Rhodes? Where were the goddamn cops?

He risked peering over at Claire Paige and caught her eyeing him in her scrap of mirror. It was impossible to tell what she was thinking, what her own fears were. His heart went out to Claire. It was his fault that they were in this mess. Sure, she had introduced the subject of the twenty grand, but she had done so in a joking fashion. It was he who had transformed the joke to a grim reality.

His head was bent again when the door opened and Kirk Mason came in.

'Hi, everybody!' Kirk greeted in his friendly way. 'I got trapped in a traffic snarl-up,' he said to Claire, his tone apologetic.

'It's all right, Kirk. Mr Otis hasn't put in an appearance yet.'

'That's a relief,' Mason grinned. 'But odd. Mr Otis doesn't usually sleep in late.'

And so the morning began. All might have been normal were it not for the absence of Hank Otis. Denton tried desperately to concentrate on what he was doing. It was utterly impossible. His mind kept churning out guesses, theories. The suspense was gradually becoming unbearable.

It was what they were waiting for, he told himself. They were biding their time, playing it the cool and patient way, waiting for something to break, for *someone* to break.

It wouldn't be he. His nerve was firm and intact. He would keep it so. He realized he was being stupidly selfish. What about Claire and her feelings? What about the torture of suspense she was going through? He longed to go over there and comfort her, urge her to hold herself together.

Her typewriter clicked away.

Jimmy Florian came in and went to Claire's desk. He had brought a sheaf of papers and Claire studied them. She said something to Jimmy and the youth went out again.

Denton glanced at his wristwatch. Thirty minutes had passed since he had sat down at his desk. He thought his watch had stopped, but it hadn't. How could he continue in this fashion until the lunch break?

He finished typing the invoices assigned to him. He rose and crossed to Claire's desk. He could see her freeze on his approach. She looked up at him, her features set, her eyes calm but wary.

'What is it, Denton?'

'I'm through with that batch of stuff,' he told her. He dropped the pitch of his voice. 'What the hell is going on, Claire?'

'I don't know,' she groaned. 'I — '

The office door opened and portly Jack Rhodes stepped through.

'Oh Claire,' he said in a tone that was crisp with curtness, 'will you come with me for a minute?'

Claire got up without answering him

and went to join him. Rhodes let her pass out in front of him and his sharp gaze ranged the room briefly. His eyes touched Denton but he didn't speak. He went out after Claire and slammed the door on his heels.

10

Claire seemed to be away for ever.

Denton had no doubt that she had been taken to the police for questioning. This was the method the bright boys had adopted. They had thrown a screen of secrecy over the murder and were working underneath it like beavers. They were banking on a quick solution and an early arrest, and then the newspapers could take the wraps off and show everybody what a set of geniuses the police were.

Denton could imagine what they were doing to Claire. They would have her in a dark room at headquarters, with a bright light shining in her face and eyes, so that she wouldn't know what day it was. If they discovered one tiny crack in her story they would keep on digging until the crack became a hole, and the crime which she and Denton had planned would be laid bare. They wouldn't stop there, either. It wasn't a robber they were after, but a robber who had turned killer. The tag would be ready-made for him when his turn came to be grilled.

He sat there and sweated, longing to get out of this building, into the air, longing to have Claire Paige with him. The hell with the twenty grand so long as he had her. Between them they would hit it off somewhere else somehow. Money wasn't everything. Freedom came first. There were guys with uncounted millions who would pour them all into the trash can if they were able to take a long walk in the fresh air.

It was Olive Overton at the bottom of it, of course. She had gone to the cops with her tale and the cops had taken it from there. After all he had told the girl, there was very little left for the police to exercise their imagination on. He had given them the case on a plate — via the cool artist shacked up in the attic apartment.

Had she squealed on him?

He nearly jumped off his chair when the office door opened and Claire entered. She was not alone. Jack Rhodes was still with her. Rhodes had her left elbow and was talking soothingly in a low voice. Claire appeared to have been crying. Her face was pale and stiff and there was a redness about her eyes. She had a handkerchief in her fingers and she dabbed at her cheeks.

She eased down on the chair at her desk. Rhodes stood beside her. He seemed deeply concerned.

'Are you sure you are all right, Claire? There's no reason why you shouldn't take the morning off.'

'No, no . . . Thank you, Mr Rhodes. I am all right. I would rather stay here.'

Their voices carried clearly just then because Sally and Kirk had stopped typing also and were staring at Rhodes and Claire as Denton was.

Jack Rhodes straightened and looked about him. He cleared his throat. His eyes came to rest on Sally Baines.

'Miss Baines, could I ask you to come with me for a few minutes?'

'Very well, Mr Rhodes.'

Sally glanced at Kirk Mason before she

crossed the floor to join her boss. They went out together. The door closed. Denton felt like smashing something to relieve his feelings. He had an almost uncontrollable urge to go to Claire and grab her into his arms. They must have been rough with her. There was no doubt they had been rough with her. But she had weathered it.

Kirk Mason was watching him, so he had to keep his feelings in check. There was frank curiosity in Kirk's gaze.

'What gives?' he said in a voice pitched for Denton's ears.

Denton shrugged, spreading his arms. He looked at Claire again. Claire had her face cupped in her hands and seemed to be studying some papers on her desk. She was paying no heed to either of them. She was locked in a world of her own.

A moment later her typewriter began clacking furiously. Kirk Mason resumed his typing. Denton forced himself to go on keeping up appearances, but it was useless. He simply had to have a word with Claire.

He grabbed a handful of invoices and

crossed to Claire's desk. He halted with his back to Kirk Mason and spoke in a voice that Mason would hear.

'There has been an error made in this order, Miss Paige.'

She stared blankly at him for several seconds. For Mason's benefit she pretended to finger through the invoices. Her fingers trembled badly, Denton noticed.

'He was murdered,' she said in a fierce whisper.

'I know. It was what I was trying to tell you. What did you say to them? It was the cops, wasn't it?'

'He was murdered, Blake. He didn't have to be murdered.'

'But, hell, I didn't do it . . . '

'Keep your voice down.'

Denton's heart was hammering frantically. Here was an angle that had never occurred to him, not seriously. Claire imagining that he had really killed old Hank!

'We've got to talk,' he hissed at her.

'Not now. Go away, Blake. Kirk is watching us.'

He was reluctant to move. But she was

right. Mason would be eyeing them, and he was sharp enough to realize there could be something going on between them.

'You did see the cops?'

'Yes, yes! Now go.'

He lifted the invoices and walked back to his desk. Mason met his gaze when he glanced at him and raised his brows questioningly. Denton just shrugged. He was mad clear through at Claire. What did she take him for — a crazy, mixed-up murderer?

★　★　★

Shortly afterwards Jack Rhodes escorted Sally Baines back to the office. Denton tensed, waiting for Rhodes to tell him to accompany him.

'Mr Mason,' Rhodes said to Kirk, 'please come with me.'

'Me, Mr Rhodes?' Mason asked in a baffled voice.

'You,' Rhodes told him. His eyes shuttled to Denton. 'We'll want you later, Blake.'

It provided him with an opening and Denton took it. He managed to drag a weak smile to his lips.

'What's going on, Mr Rhodes?'

Jack Rhodes' expression was worried and harassed. He started to say something, bit it off, and made a gesture with his head for Kirk to follow him.

'You'll hear soon enough, Blake,' was all he said.

He went on out with Kirk Mason and slammed the door behind him. Sally was walking slowly to her desk and she paused to look at Denton. Her eyes were wide with shock.

'You'll never guess what has happened, Blake — ' she began.

Claire Paige interrupted her.

'Please, Sally,' she said sternly. 'You were given instructions, were you not?'

'Yes, I was, Miss Paige.' Sally stood her ground behind Denton's chair, showing a streak of rebellion that was entirely new in her. 'But what's the reason for all the secrecy? If they don't want us to talk about it they should have kept us apart. Mr Otis is dead, Blake,' she went on in a strained voice. 'He was murdered last night. Right there in his office!'

'What!' Denton cried, simulating horrified astonishment.

'Sally, will you please go to your desk?' Claire Paige snapped angrily at her.

'I'm going,' Sally retorted. 'But why are they questioning us? Do they think that one of us killed him?'

'Take it easy,' Denton said, coming out of his chair and putting an arm about her shoulders. He could see the girl was on the verge of hysterics. He led her across to her desk. Seated, Sally Baines covered her face in her hands and her shoulders began shaking as she sobbed convulsively.

Denton remained with her until she calmed down. He would feel the weight of Claire's eyes on his back. There was something about Claire's manner that was frightening. She was too cold, too collected. But likely it was her only defence and she had to make the best of it.

He returned to his own desk presently. Claire had given up pretence of working and was sitting, shoulders squared and stiff looking straight ahead of her. Sally's typewriter started clacking spasmodically.

There was a dull, empty sensation in the pit of Denton's stomach now. Sally Baines was right. Why take them out separately to be grilled when they were turned back into the office afterwards? Why leave him to the last for questioning? He knew why. They were hoping that his nerve was commencing to crack, that by the time it was his turn for the hot seat he would be in such a state of the jitters he would disintegrate and make a full confession on the spot. But his nerve wouldn't crack and he would not disintegrate. He hadn't murdered Hank Otis and that was that. He had no intention of making any sort of confession, so Rhodes and the cops and everyone else concerned could go to hell and hunt for the real killer.

If Olive Overton hadn't squealed on him.

Kirk Mason was absent for longer than Claire and Sally had been. He came back finally, walking into the office in front of Jack Rhodes. Kirk looked as though he had been through a tornado.

'Come along, Blake.'

'Sure, Mr Rhodes.'

He rose and went to join Rhodes. Going past Claire's desk he shot a glance at her, but she averted her head to obviate having to look at him.

The door closed on them, Denton wheeled to Jack Rhodes.

'Sally told us, Mr Rhodes. She couldn't help it. Something happened to Mr Otis last night?'

'Yes,' Rhodes returned in a steely voice. 'But I can't talk about it. Follow me, Denton.'

Denton followed him, noting how he had been called Denton and not Blake or even Mr Denton. A lump of ice lodged against his spine. He had the feeling of being on his way to the death house.

Jack Rhodes led him along the corridor linking the wing of the building where he worked with the wing where Rhodes had his own private office. Everything seemed very quiet in the building. There was a tense hush as if all action was being held in abeyance until a weighty problem was solved.

Rhodes halted at the door leading to his quarters. Denton had never been in there. He had never been in this wing of the building at all.

'Go ahead, Denton,' Rhodes told him.

Denton gripped the door handle and twisted it. He looked sideways at the portly man.

'Police?'

'Please do as you're told,' Jack Rhodes snapped. It was plain his own nerves were on edge. He might have more worry on his shoulders than that of the death of his partner. Waterman and his watches flitted through Dentons brain.

He twisted the handle of the door and entered the room.

★ ★ ★

It was an office slightly larger than the one Hank Otis had used. There was a desk, three chairs besides the swivel chair opposite the desk, a bank of filing cabinets, a shelf with a few dust-covered books lying drunkenly on it.

Seated at the desk was a big man in a

grey suit. He was lying back in the chair with a pipe jutting from the side of his narrow, tight mouth. He had blue eyes that bit into Denton with the sharpness of ice-picks.

There was another big man standing with his back against the wall. He was wide-shouldered and rugged looking. He was wearing a brown suit with a white shirt that had gone soft with heat and sweat, and was curling up at the collar tips. He eyed Denton with frank curiosity.

'You're Blake Denton?' the man at the desk demanded flatly.

'That's right. But what is this all in aid of. I — '

'You'll find out. Sit down. You can smoke if you want.'

'Thanks.' Denton took a chair that put him directly opposite the big man and with his back to the one leaning against the wall. A sickening jolt fisted into his stomach, but it passed and he made an effort to pull himself together.

'My name is Granger, Mr Denton. Lieutenant Granger. I'm attached to the homicide squad here in town. That is

Sergeant Ed Raven. Now . . . ' He lowered his eyes to a sheet of paper in front of him, removed his pipe from his mouth and laid it on a conveniently placed ashtray. 'You're Blake Denton, with an address at eight, four, six, Ethna Road. Right?'

'That's right. But what — '

'Take it easy, Denton, will you.' Granger shot him a hard look. 'I'll do the talking and when I'm through you can do the talking. Right?'

Denton just shrugged and said nothing. He had the feeling he was caught in a net and the cops were in the process of hauling in their catch. What he must do was concentrate on the questions that would be fired at him, examine them carefully but swiftly, and answer them in the best fashion to serve his own interests.

'Do you know why you're here, Denton?' Granger said.

'I didn't know until a short time ago. Sally came back to the office and nearly went to pieces. She said Mr Otis had been murdered in his office last night.'

'It was the first you heard of it?'

'It certainly was. You might as well try to get water out of a stone as news out of Miss Paige. So it isn't just a gag then? It's really true? Mr Otis was murdered last night?'

'Right,' Granger said slowly and picked up his pipe. He fumbled in the pockets of his coat until he found his tobacco pouch. He began pushing fresh tobacco in on top of the ashy dottle. He glanced across Denton's right shoulder at Raven. 'Lend me your lighter, Ed.'

'You can have mine,' Denton said and reached to his jacket.

'It's okay. I'll borrow Sergeant Raven's. Thanks, Ed.' He took the butane lighter that came over Denton's right shoulder, used it to puff his pipe up the way he wanted it going. He laid the lighter on the desk in front of him.

Sweat started oozing on to Denton's forehead.

'Is this going to run for long?'

'There's no telling,' Granger said gruffly. 'Why should you worry?' He smiled bleakly. 'While you're resting you're not working. We have Mr Rhodes' full approval. Now, Denton, where did you spend your time last night?'

'Me? You've got to be kidding, Lieutenant! I didn't murder Hank Otis. I didn't —'

'Shut up,' Ed Raven said behind him. 'Keep your lip buttoned until you're asked a question. When you're asked a question, answer it. Don't elaborate. Don't run off at irrelevant tangents. You're not being charged with anything, buddy. Just cooperate, will you?'

'Sure,' Denton said weakly. 'Sure. But I've got a right to stake my claim. I didn't murder Hank Otis.'

'Where were you last night, Denton?' Granger asked him. He puffed gently at his pipe. His eyes never left Denton's face.

'At home,' Denton said.

'All night?' Granger probed.

'Depending on what you mean by night. Early on I drove into town. Drove around for a while. Had a few drinks.'

'You don't have a girl friend?'

The query came at Denton like a knife thrust. How exactly should he answer? What precisely did these police officers know?

'I haven't got a steady girl friend, if that's what you mean. I take a dame out occasionally. But I never stay stuck with one for longer than a few days at a time. I guess I'm not the type to make good marriageable material.'

'Were you with a girl last night?'

Denton shook his head.

'No, I wasn't. Like I said, I drove around town for a while, had a couple of drinks, then went home.'

'What time did you get home?'

'I'm not sure. It could have been eleven, eleven-thirty.'

'What did you do then?' Granger asked him.

'Nothing. I read a book for a little, watched TV for an hour. I went to bed around twelve-thirty or one o'clock.'

'And you didn't go out again? You're quite sure that you didn't?'

This was it, Denton thought bitterly. Someone at the apartment house had heard him leave at one-thirty, or seen him drive off in his car. Or Olive Overton had given them her version of the night's events . . .

He had taken the step and it would be fatal to retrace it.

'I didn't go out again until this morning,' he told Granger.

'Okay, Denton,' Granger said. He opened a drawer in Jack Rhodes' desk and extracted a snub-nosed .38. He placed it on the desk between them. 'You ever see this gun before?'

'Yeah, I did see it. As a matter of fact I handled it yesterday.'

'When?'

'I rode shotgun to the bank with Mr Otis. He was drawing cash and he took me along to act as guard.'

'You saw what Otis drew at the bank?'

'I checked the amount for him. Twenty thousand dollars.'

'Why did he need twenty thousand in cash?'

Denton shrugged.

'Why ask me? I don't have a clue.'

'You knew the dough would be locked up in Otis' safe?'

'I didn't know what he intended doing with it.'

'But you guessed it would be in his

safe?' Granger persisted.

'I wasn't interested in guessing. It wasn't my money and it didn't concern me what he did with it.'

'You returned the gun to Otis when you got back from the bank?'

'Yes, I did.'

'Otis was shot with this gun, Denton. How about that.'

'I didn't shoot him. I didn't steal the money.'

'Who said the money had been stolen?'

Denton went hot and cold.

'Nobody. I'm just figuring the money was stolen.'

Granger pushed the gun away in the drawer. He closed the drawer. He made a short motion with his head. He sighed.

'Okay, Denton. That's all for now. You can go.'

Denton's legs were rubbery as he rose and left the room.

11

At the lunch hour there was an opportunity to compare notes with Kirk Mason in the Pollard Street diner. Mason simply couldn't get over the shock of Hank Otis having been murdered.

'It makes you wonder what the hell everything is about, Blake,' he said to Denton. 'I mean, I'm not what you would call a deep thinker, but it makes you look at things differently, somehow. One minute Mr Otis was there, and the next — Well, I ask you. It could happen to anybody, Blake.'

'Sure, sure,' Denton said impatiently. He wasn't interested in the wonder of life and death. There were other things more important and urgent to be concerned about. 'What did the cops say to you, Kirk?'

Mason had trouble remembering in exact detail what the homicide lieutenant had said to him. For him the questioning had been incidental and fundamentally irrelevant. Hank Otis was dead. He had been murdered. At first he had thought he was under suspicion by the police, but then he saw how ridiculous the idea was and he had soon dismissed it. What had the most impact for him was wrapped up in clearly defined physical terms. Hank Otis had been alive, but now he was dead. He had been there but now he wasn't there.

Denton could have grabbed Mason by the shirt front and shaken him.

'They asked you to give an account of your movements last night?'

'Yes, they did.' Mason laughed shortly. 'If they could have seen me sitting up with Louella and plying her with pills and hot drinks they would have known without asking. I had a real bastard of a night last night, Blake.'

'I'm sorry to hear it,' Denton said. He had no appetite for the food before him and merely picked half-heartedly at it. 'They asked you if you knew about the twenty thousand dollars in Hank's safe?'

'Sure. It's the reason the old guy was

killed. I told them how I'd gone to the bank a few times before with Mr Otis to draw the money. I said I knew the gun and had handled it. They asked why he took you yesterday instead of me.'

'That's what bugs me,' Denton said with a grim smile. 'Hank said you were busy. Where you that busy?'

'I'm always busy, Blake. But here, they didn't suspect you of going after the dough?'

Denton had bother meeting Mason's eyes. He shrugged.

'How can you say? I knew he had drawn the dough. I knew he had locked it in the safe. I guess that makes me a candidate for the cops' short list.'

'Horse feathers, Blake. They would never suspect you. No, I'm convinced they believe it was an outside job. They're just going through the motions of questioning the staff in order to eliminate us. Still, you've got to admit it's a bit of a mystery. Who else knew the dough would be there? And what brought the old guy to the office in the middle of the night, anyhow?'

Denton shook his head. Talking with Kirk wasn't going to solve anything. It was Claire he needed to talk with. She may have some ideas on the subject. She had headed off on her own at one o'clock, going swiftly from the building as though she feared he would try to stop her.

He had to talk to her, had to knock the notion from her mind that he might have slain Hank.

On returning to the warehouse with Kirk Mason, he told Kirk to carry on without him.

'I want to take a minute to look at my car,' he said. 'It seemed to be mis-firing this morning.

'Could be a bad plug. Or the fuel pump.' Mason strolled on through the front door and Denton gravitated to the Volkswagen.

Claire's car was not on the parking area, which meant she had not returned from lunch yet. There were no police cars parked either, but it didn't mean anything one way or the other. The cops might be back in force after the lunch break.

At two o'clock there was still no sign of

Claire, and Denton went on up to the office. He had just seated himself at his desk when the office door opened and Claire Paige entered. It was as if she had deliberately hung back until she knew he would have resumed work. The thought nagged him like an angry boil.

The afternoon dragged as Denton never remembered one dragging. Try as he did to concentrate he found it impossible. He had the sensation of a trap being weaved about him. Although he couldn't see the machination in action he had the conviction it was there, nevertheless. Had Claire deliberately picked on him to act as a stooge, to manipulate him into a situation where he would emerge as the fall guy, while the man who had really killed Hank Otis and stolen the twenty thousand was high and dry in the shadows?

He refused to believe this was so. Claire had proved to him what she thought of him and how she felt about him. Claire was as anxious to go away somewhere with him as he was anxious to go away with her.

What was the answer then?

He would have to be calm and patient, have to wait and see.

At four o'clock Jack Rhodes came into the office and asked for their attention. As he spoke all eyes focused on the stout man. An air of tension dominated the room.

'Thank you for cooperating with the police,' he said. 'I'm sorry to involve innocent people, but you'll understand it was necessary. Mr Otis was murdered and his murderer will have to be found and brought to justice.'

'Do the police have a lead, Mr Rhodes?'

Speaking the question, Denton felt the eyes of the others switching to him. Claire had swivelled on her chair and was watching him with a blank gaze.

'That I cannot say, Blake. When it comes to murder they play things close to the chest. But I am sure you are under no more suspicion than anyone else.'

'But — ' Denton began, his face turning red.

'Yes, yes, I know, Blake,' Rhodes

interrupted him. 'You accompanied Mr Otis to the bank yesterday. You saw the money come back here. You knew it was being deposited in Mr Otis' safe. Therefore, you're bound to feel more edgy than the rest of us. But you needn't be, Blake. I'm sure that everybody here knew how Mr Otis has gone through the same performance in the past. I warned him against leaving money in his safe overnight. He did this to meet the whim of a somewhat eccentric salesman. Mr Probart does a line in home-produced perfumes that sell well with us. But Probart was badly let down by a warehouse once, and ever since demands ready cash . . . '

Probart? What the hell was he talking about, Denton wondered. Was this in the nature of an exercise in white-washing to cover up for the deals in watches? For Probart read Waterman?

He glanced at Claire, but she evaded his eyes.

'I thought the salesman was called Waterman,' he blurted out to Rhodes.

'Waterman? Where did you hear that,

Blake? We don't deal with anyone called Waterman.'

'Oh! I guess I heard wrong. But what brought Mr Otis to his office last night?'

Rhodes paled a little and he pulled at his heavy jowls.

'It seems,' he began and stopped. He cleared his throat and continued, his attention rivetted on Denton. 'It seems Mr Otis had a notion that an attempt might be made to rob the safe last night. It's what his wife says. Mrs Otis told me that Hank — Mr Otis — made this excuse for getting out of bed and driving to the warehouse. He didn't drive himself, naturally. He didn't care for driving. He called a taxi cab — '

'Then the driver of the cab might have seen something suspicious. Did it occur to the police to check on the cab drivers?'

'Really, Blake!' Rhodes smothered a meagre smile. 'You seem to have some of the qualitites that go towards making a good detective. Still, you make a valid point and I appreciate it. Yes, the police have checked the local cab companies. They found the driver who picked up Mr

Otis at his home. Unfortunately, the instructions the driver received were to drop Mr Otis at the warehouse and call back in half an hour to collect him.'

Denton shrugged and mustered a weak grin. He looked sheepish.

'It was unfortunate. Forgive me for running off at the mouth, Mr Rhodes.'

'It's okay, Blake. I admire the way your brain works.'

Shortly after that Rhodes left the office. The door closing on him was a signal for Kirk Mason to make a humorous gibe at Denton.

'Smart thinking, old son! You may have taken a step up the ladder of success at *Advance*.'

Denton laughed gruffly.

'Go stand on your head,' he said. He looked at Claire. Claire had been watching his reflection in her scrap of mirror and she dropped her eyes quickly.

Denton reflected that he might have behaved recklessly just then. But at least he had learned why there had been no car parked at the warehouse last night on his arrival. Old Hank had used a cab and given the cabbie orders to drive off and return for him later. Whatever else it indicated, it pointed to Hank having felt uneasy about the money in his safe. Hank may have suspected someone of having his eye on the money. Who? Had he guessed that he and Claire were planning to steal it? It didn't seem possible.

There was one other angle to be considered. Hank's reason for making the trip to the warehouse may have been a relatively innocent one. Yes, he might have been uneasy about leaving twenty thousand dollars locked up in the office safe overnight, but his reason for journeying to the warehouse could have been, simply, to collect the money and keep it at home until morning. Only, in that event, would he not have told the cabbie to wait for him?

Denton spent the rest of the afternoon in examining theory after theory. He was glad when five o'clock came round and it was time to jack up work for the day and go home.

He didn't go home directly. He stopped off at a bar to have a drink. He had the notion that Lieutenant Granger might pin a tail to him. He couldn't see a tail, but it didn't have to mean it wasn't there.

He sat at the counter for some thirty minutes, and then, cigarette in lips, he stepped into a phone booth and called Claire Paige's apartment.

Claire answered after a brief moment's wait.

'Hello,' she said. 'This is — '

'This is me, honey,' Denton broke in on her. 'I thought it would be sensible not to follow you home. But I've got to see you soon, Claire.'

'You can't come here, Blake,' she said with a catch in her voice. 'It would be the height of stupidity. I saw a strange man sitting in a car in front of the apartment building. He could be a detective.'

Denton whistled softly.

'What did he look like? Tall? Wearing a soft felt hat with a snapped-down brim?'

'You've got a tall man on the brain! How do I know if he was tall? But, yes I suppose he was. He was wearing a soft hat. He — '

'What kind of a car was it?' Denton

rasped at her. It was a queer time to be making wisecracks. Also, there was a quality in the girl's tone which rubbed him the wrong way.

'An old Buick. Well, not that old. Three or four years. A dark colour. Dusty.'

'Oh,' Denton said. 'Yes, it could be a cop Claire.'

'There might be one outside your front door also, Blake.'

He told her he didn't know if there was or not. He was having a drink in a bar before going to Ethna Road. But cops apart, he would have to see her shortly. What time would she like him to visit?

'It would be silly for you to come here at all, Blake.'

'You can come to me . . . '

'No. Look, we'd better meet outside somewhere. You know where the Grove movie theatre is on Christy Avenue?'

'Yeah, I do. But this is no time to sit through a movie, honey.'

'We're not going to sit through a movie,' she replied sharply. 'I'll drive there at around eight-thirty. I'll leave my car on the parking area and buy a ticket for the show. I'll come out by the rear exit and walk back to the street. You pick me up on the street. But you'd better make sure you aren't being followed.'

'Nice thinking, Claire. Okay, honey. See you at about eight-forty.'

She broke the connection before he did. He replaced the receiver, stood deep in thought for several seconds, then left the booth.

He had another drink at the bar and went into the street to collect the Volkswagen and drive home.

There were no strange vehicles parked in the vicinity of his apartment building on his arrival there. He sat for a while in his car, puffing on a cigarette and giving a possible tail the time it would take to drive into the street behind him. Satisfied that the coast was clear, he alighted and went up to his apartment.

He made a pot of black coffee and drank three cups of the hot liquid. His brain was still racing at top speed, but instead of following a direct and meaningful course it was tearing around in circles, like a dog, trapped in a maze, that couldn't find its way out.

Denton showered later and ran his electric shaver over his jaws. He put on brown slacks, a lightweight sweater, and brown sports jacket, and by eight o'clock he was ready to keep his rendezvous with Claire at the Grove movie house.

He left early enough to give him the opportunity of driving to Christy Avenue by a roundabout route. There was no sign of a car following him and he began to relax somewhat. The strange man at the Biltmore apartment block might not have been a cop at all. The situation being what it was, Claire could be forgiven for imagining the police were keeping tabs on her. Had there really been a stranger as she had described, or had she dreamed up the trick to keep him away from her apartment?

He didn't know. There was no way of telling. He knew a little about Claire, but not a lot. There could be depths to the girl's personality he was unaware of. He hated having to view her through shadows of suspicion, but it would be stupid not to acknowledge facts as they revealed themselves.

He saw her as he cruised along Christy Avenue. She was wearing a dark outfit and had a scarf tied about her head. He braked and opened the off-side door to let her in. She slammed the door after her and panted fearfully.

'Get moving fast, Blake.'

'What's the matter? Are you — ?'

'A man came into the theatre on my heels. He took a seat directly behind me. I'm sure he followed me out.'

Denton glanced at her. He pressed his foot down on the gas pedal and the Volkswagen roared off. He peered in the rear view mirror but could see nothing in the road behind him.

'Are you sure?'

'I said I was. Just keep driving.'

There was a sobering crispness in the peremptory way she snapped the order. Denton swung left at the end of the avenue, went through traffic lights at the red. He kept going along Market Street, turned left again at the First Avenue intersection, and sped up the crowded thoroughfare, intent on making for the

Wheeler underpass and the western suburbs.

Beside him, Claire Paige gasped harshly.

'Be careful. If you have a smash-up we'll really be in trouble.'

'According to you we are in trouble, baby,' he said thinly. He added quickly, 'Why the big interest in you, do you suppose?'

'How the hell should I know?'

He threw her a brief stare. One surprise after another! This was more like the ice-berg when the spring crack-up came. The dame was tough and brittle the whole way through.

They said nothing until the business zone was in their rear and they were curving round an expensive residential district. The girl had been watching the back window of the car and now she sank down and shuddered.

'My nerves will never stand this.'

'I don't see what you're grumbling about,' Denton said tersely. 'If anyone's nerves are taking a beating it's mine. I'm the guy who broke into the joint, you know.'

'Don't tell me! I was mad to have anything to do with it. I was mad to mention the money to you . . . '

'Here, here! Less of the bitterness stuff. We did it and it's done. At this stage we've got to keep our control. Panic will get us no place, Claire. What we must do is talk it over, try and figure out what went wrong.'

'What went wrong?' Her voice had risen to a fine, despairing screech. 'If it wasn't so tragic I could laugh at you, Blake. You made a mess of it. You bungled it. But what did you do with the money? Did you manage to get it to Fosset's woods?'

'What the hell are you talking about?' he raged. They were clear of the suburbs now and boring into a flat stretch of sand and shrubbery. 'What money? I didn't get the money.'

'You didn't get the money!' she echoed. 'But you said on the phone. Maybe I was too confused to think clearly. But if Mr Otis walked in on you and you murdered him, how did you fail to get the twenty thousand that was in the safe?'

12

Denton braked the car to a snarling standstill.

The narrow road was deserted, so they had it to themselves. A fury rose in him such as he had never experienced, and it required all of his self-control to prevent him grabbing the girl by the throat and shaking her silly.

'What the hell are you raving about, Claire? I didn't murder Hank. I told you on the phone that I didn't. Were you not paying attention to what I said?'

For a moment she sat there, staring at him, her mouth partly open, her eyes wide and oscillating frantically over his face.

'If you didn't kill him, who did?' she demanded hoarsely. 'Look, Blake,' she went on swiftly, 'this is Claire talking to you and not the police. You can drop your guard. You can drop the lies — '

'Lies! But I'm not lying, damn it. Why

can't you give me the chance to explain before throwing me into the condemned cell? You take me for a complete stupe, for a heartless killer. You've got this deal by the wrong end, Claire.'

'But — but — ' Suddenly she dropped her head and covered her face with her hands. She sobbed as though she would never stop crying.

Her tears softened Denton. After all, what had he expected her to conclude in the circumstances? She knew he had gone to Hank Otis' office to steal the money. She knew that Hank had turned up there and been murdered. Who else could have murdered Hank if not he?

'I'm sorry, honey . . . '

He took her in his arms and brought her cheek against his own. Warm tears trickled down his jaws. At first she resisted him, but then she yielded to his caresses. When his mouth claimed hers he found the lips hot and moist and straining with hunger.

A moment later she pushed him away from her. She laughed shakily.

'Take it easy, Blake. This isn't the time

for losing our heads. We've got to talk, to work it out. You've got to tell me everything that happened from when you entered the warehouse.'

He told her. He explained how he had gained Hank's private office without incident.

'The door was closed and I opened it. I was using my flashlight and it picked out the safe. I saw nothing else. I took a step into the office and bam!'

'You — you mean you were knocked out?'

'Yeah,' he said tautly. 'I couldn't have been out for more than a few minutes. When I came to, the flash had rolled under a chair. I moved to lift it. My shoe touched a body. There's no sense in relating all the gory details. But by then the safe had been opened and the briefcase taken. Hank was on the floor, dead. His gun was lying beside him. I was trying to cope with everything when I heard the police sirens — '

'But how did the police know to go there, Blake?'

'How? Tell me. I don't know, Claire. All

I can do is make a guess. The killer must have phoned in to them. Or the hack driver who brought Hank to the warehouse smelt a rat and called them. I don't think he did. My money is on the killer. He figured he had hit me harder than he did. He figured I would be crawling back to consciousness by the time the cops came up.'

'But who, Blake? Who would have done it? Who else knew the money was there? How did it happen that we and the killer got the same idea on the same night?'

Denton shrugged and shook his head. Claire's face was a pale, strained mask. Her eyes glowed on him like frightened stars. Some of the doubts he had been entertaining concerning her came back to nag at him.

'I wish I had the answers, Claire.'

'Would — would Kirk have done it, Blake? After all, Kirk knew the money was in the safe. He might be in a spot financially, what with his sick wife and everything. But surely the police . . . '

'Sure. The police will have gone into the angle. If they suspect Kirk they'll follow up quickly enough, ask him if he is financially embarrassed, ask him if he managed to get his hands on a key to the front door — '

'They asked me about my key, Blake,' she broke in there.

'Yeah? What did they ask you?'

'Just if I had a key. I'm sure Mr Rhodes had already told them I carried one. I said I had. Next they asked me if I knew the combination of the safe. I said I did.'

'Do you figure they suspect you?'

She moved her shoulders fractionally.

'They'll suspect everybody until they find the killer and the money that was stolen.'

'That's another thing,' Denton said. 'The money. According to you, the money was to pay a guy called Waterman for a parcel of stolen or smuggled watches. According to Jack Rhodes, it was to pay for a parcel of home-grown perfume being delivered by an eccentric called Probart.'

'Yes, I know. It was a cover-up, naturally. Mr Rhodes wished to bluff the police.'

'That or Rhodes didn't know what Otis was trading in on the side.'

'Yes,' Claire said after a moment. 'You could be right, Blake. I don't know. But it doesn't alter the basic fact. You haven't told me how you succeeded in getting out of the building in front of the police.'

At this stage he was uncertain about how much he should tell her. One part of his mind said he could trust her completely; another part insisted she wasn't to be trusted. If she was a phoney and he told her how Olive Overton had helped him it might place the other girl in danger.

'Go on, Blake. What are you waiting for?'

He began by telling her how he had left the *Advance* building by the fire escape. From there he had gone over the roofs. It had been a rough passage while it lasted, but he had reached the ground again along the street. Then he had made a detour to reach his car.

'You left it on Felmoy Avenue?'

'Lucky for me that I did. Once in the

car I headed for home. Then I rang
you . . . '

'And that was all?'

'It wasn't enough?'

Her eyes stared at him through the
gloom. It was difficult to guess what she
was thinking. His account of the chase
across the rooftops had come over bald
and flat to his own ears. It had sounded
like a story dreamed up on the spur of the
moment. Without all the essential details
it had lacked punch.

'Blake, you — you wouldn't tell me a
lie?'

His stomach lurched and his heart
thudded steadily against his ribs. When he
spoke his voice was a thin and reedy rasp.

'You don't believe me. You don't want
to believe me. You — '

'No, Blake! Please don't say those things.
I want to believe you. I want to trust you.
But consider the stark facts . . . '

'I have considered them,' he said hollowly.
'I wandered into a deal that stinks to high
heaven. No, don't stop me, honey,' he
urged when she laid a hand on his arm.
'It's on my chest like a ton of concrete

and I won't have any peace until I get rid of it.'

She seemed to shrivel up before him. She caught her breath.

'What — what do you mean?'

'I mean frame, baby. What else would you call it? I walked into a frame. I'm not saying you contrived it, but I am saying somebody contrived it — '

'And I was part of it?' she challenged coldly. 'It's what you're trying to say, Blake. If it is, then be a man and come right out with it.'

For a tense moment they sat, eyeing each other, neither of them willing to concede an inch. Finally a harsh laugh was wrenched from Denton. He stretched his hands out to touch her, but she retreated until she was up against the door of the car.

'Don't do it Blake . . . '

'Hell, I'm sorry baby. We're on edge. We grabbed the wrong end of a hot poker. We're in the dark and until we see some light we're going to suspect each other.'

'Not me, Blake,' she said vibrantly. 'Not

me. It was a mistake from the beginning. One of us has got to keep his sense of proportion. We've got to quit seeing each other. It's too dangerous. Far, far too dangerous. If the police even suspect collusion between us we'll both be sunk. I don't want to sink. I've worked in that place for two years and I can go on working there for another two if needs be. I'd rather spend my days tied to a desk than locked up in a prison cell.'

He knew she meant it. He had the firm conviction that she meant it. He had the eerie feeling of having gone through this scene before, in a different existence, on another plane of consciousness. In a minute from now a police car would come storming down the road behind them. He began to sweat. He started up the engine.

'Where are you going?'

'Back to town.'

'But, Blake . . . '

'Yeah?' he said bleakly, foot hovering over the accelerator. 'You were talking about a prison cell.'

'Please forget it.'

'I'll try.'

He was silent on the journey back to Maxwell. He drove as though he had the car to himself. Claire Paige kept looking at him occasionally. Twice her mouth opened to say something, but whatever she had in mind it went unsaid. They were approaching Christy Avenue when she spoke at last.

'What did you do with the duplicate key?'

'I got rid of it. I had a shovel and I got rid of that. If you think I used the shovel you could always drive to Fosset's woods and dig around.'

He heard her breath escape slowly from her lips. If he'd hurt her it was because he wanted to hurt her. He saw everything they had had going dissolving into ruin. If she wasn't wholly to blame she was at least partly to blame. She ought to have trusted him. She ought to have had faith in him. All she was interested in just then was the safety of her own skin. She didn't have to worry.

He braked to a halt in the vicinity of the movie theatre and told her to get out.

'I'm — I'm sorry, Blake.'

'Don't be sorry for me, honey. I can look after myself.'

She gave him a long stare before slipping to the road and slamming the car door behind her. Denton drove off, not glancing to right or left. A foul mood was on him and he knew only one method of appeasing it.

He drove to a bar and had a few drinks. He sat for a while and smoked, snubbing a garrulous character on the neighbouring stool. The guy was fat, thick-shouldered and tough looking. He sneered at Denton with his heavy lips.

'What'sa matter, palsy? You just naturally a mean joe or playing hard to get?'

Denton shook his head but said nothing. He killed his cigarette and ordered another scotch on the rocks.

'Make it a double.'

'You're gonna finish up on a slab,' the fat character said. 'You're gonna drink yourself to death, palsy.'

'That right,' Denton said vaguely.

The fat guy laughed and poked a finger into Denton's ribs.

'You mean you don't care? You had a spat with your wife? I wouldn't drink myself to death on account of any woman. They're not worth it, palsy.'

'Go away,' Denton told him. His drink came and he paid. He had the glass to his mouth when the fat character jabbed his ribs again, causing him to spill some of the liquor. Denton looked at him. He saw beefy jowls that needed shaving and two rows of teeth that needed dental treatment.

'What'sa matter, Joe?'

'Nothing. Quit sticking your paws into my side.'

'You wanna make something out of it?'

Denton groaned. The fat guy was off his stool, his cleft chin jutting belligerently. The bartender was signalling to somebody in the rear of the bar. The fat guy swung a meaty fist at Denton. Denton moved his head in time but the bunched knuckles burned the edge of his right ear.

Denton hit him. It was a piledriver of a punch that carried all of his misery and bitterness. It smashed the fat character's nose into a bloody mess and put him on his back on the floor.

Denton stood looking down at him for several seconds. He heard feet scuffling and stared dazedly at a crew-cut roust-about.

'Out,' he ordered in a thin, clipped voice.

'But I didn't — '

'Out, friend. I mean you. I mean now. I haven't got any more speech to spare on you.'

'Then the hell with you,' Denton growled and headed for the door.

He stood on the dark street and dragged air to his lungs. He had a desire to turn about and go in there and pull the entire joint around their ears.

He shrugged and walked to his car. He didn't notice the car that drew away from the curb in his wake. By the time he reached Ethna Road and his apartment house the trailing car was a mere ten yards behind him.

He locked the Volkswagen and went up to his apartment. He was closing the door when he looked down and saw a large shoe planted in the opening. His eyes lifted to the hard features of the man who had been leaning against the wall in Jack Rhodes' office.

'You,' he muttered, his heart sinking.

'Ed Raven, Denton. Remember? Can I come in?'

'What do you want?' A shaft of ice had laid itself along Denton's spine, curdling the blood in his veins.

'Just to come in. To talk. Are you afraid to talk to me, Denton?'

Denton drew the door open and jerked his head. He was trying to think clearly through the liquor fumes. For how long had Raven been sitting on his tail? Had he seen Claire Paige get out of his car on Christy Avenue?

Ed Raven strolled into the living room.

He seated himself on a straight-backed chair and Denton slumped down on a lounging chair opposite him. Denton began searching for cigarettes, but Raven beat him to it, extracting a pack from his pocket, shaking up two cigarettes and giving him one of them. Raven leaned across to let him draw a light from a silver-plated lighter. Their eyes met. The detective grinned faintly.

'You've taken on a load. Do you do it every night? I mean, you must have trouble getting out for work in the mornings with a thick head.'

'I don't drink every night. Look, Raven, I'm not drunk. I'm not backward, either. I've got a hunch you figure I'm the guy who murdered old Hank.'

Raven's eyes clouded momentarily. He stared at the tip of his cigarette, then he stared at Denton. His features were humourless and hard.

'So we don't pull our punches?' he said. 'It's how I like it, Denton. Talk straight from the shoulder goes a long way with me. Okay then. Let me give you something straight. If I figured you had murdered Hank Otis I wouldn't be talking to you here in your front room.'

'You suspect me then?'

'Yeah, I do Denton.' Raven looked massive sitting on the small chair. He crossed one leg over the other. 'But not only you. His partner could have done it. The guy Kirk could have done it. Or either of the dames. Oh, don't tell me about dames, friend. I've seen them in action. Listened to them flap their mouths around. What I'm getting at is this,' Raven continued in a conversational fashion, 'for my money you're the boy. You look like you could make like a cat over a bunch of rooftops. You look like a boy who could scream each time you walk into that place in the morning. Twenty thousand bucks isn't the top of the world. But it would provide a starter, a grubstake, if you want. Get it? It's what makes you so attractive to me, Denton.'

Denton slumped back in his chair and looked at him. He took a drag from Raven's cigarette, but the cigarette seemed flavoured with the lawman's personality. He pushed it into an ashbowl at his elbow. He wished he hadn't drunk so much.

'I think I get your point, mister,' he said coolly. 'I don't blame you for what you think about me. I don't blame you for wanting to pin me down. But I didn't kill Hank Otis. I didn't steal the dough.'

'That's all you've got to say? I mean, if

you make it easy for me I can do something along the lines of making it easy for you. It might be your only opportunity, buster. A clean breast could give you a clean sheet. You've nothing more to say?'

Denton shook his head.

'I didn't do it.'

Ed Raven rose and moved to the door. He paused there to look back at Denton.

'Sleep on it, friend. By morning you could have different ideas on the subject. Oh, I nearly forgot.' He opened the door and Denton saw two other plainclothes cops standing there. 'Come ahead, boys,' Raven told them. 'Give the whole joint the full treatment. If you're innocent you don't have anything to hide, Denton. You don't mind if we search?'

Denton shook his head again. The two detectives came into the room. They didn't bother glancing in his direction. They began searching the apartment. He knew that other cops would be down in the street, going over the Volkswagen.

He felt trapped.

13

He sat in a sort of stupor after they had gone.

They had not found anything incriminating, of course. He was of the opinion that Raven had not expected to find anything that would point a finger at him. It had all been an elaborate act — a chest-thumping exercise designed to confuse him and put him off his guard.

He prided himself on having weathered it. It would take more than a dumb-ox cop with big feet and thick neck to knock him out of stride.

Who did he think he was kidding? Raven hadn't come to the apartment because he was bored with the monotony of his existence. He had come equipped with at least one solid reason, and perhaps a whole array of solid reasons. The cop was nobody's fool. He didn't go around making ominous noises for the kicks he got out of it.

No, he couldn't underestimate Ed Raven or any of the other men engaged on the case. He would be a fool to imagine he could come out winner in a game of cops and robbers.

'*Sleep on it, friend. By morning you could have different ideas on the subject.*'

Denton sought for subtle undercurrents of meaning in the statement. Did Raven — or his lieutenant — guess that two people had planned the robbery, and that a little delicate pressure applied to the right nerve centre might bear fruit in the shape of a squeal?

It was inevitable that he should think of Olive Overton once more and ask himself yet again if she had in any way aligned herself against him.

He gave up beating his brain finally. If he was on a spot then he was on a spot. There was only one effective remedy to swing the limelight from him. Get to the bottom of the gag. In other words, find out who really had murdered Hank Otis and taken off with the money. Whoever it was had left him to face the music. Therefore he had licence and obligation to root the guy out. Did he have the capability?

He went to the bathroom and held his head under the sink faucet. The cold water dispersed a lot of the cobwebs clouding his thoughts. Then he lit a cigarette and sat down by the phone.

He rang Claire Paige's apartment. It was a big risk to run but he just had to do it. Waiting, he glanced at his wristwatch. The time was drawing on to midnight. There was no answer to his call and he wondered where she had gone to from the Christy Avenue parking lot.

He would wait for a while and ring again later. Then an idea occurred to him and he brought over the directory. Olive Overton's number was listed in the yellow pages under *Commercial Artists*. It was another risk to take but he felt it would be worth it.

A few seconds passed and then the girl answered him.

'Fleetwood double two, double six. Yes, who is it?'

'It's me, Olive. There's no one there, is there?'

'Mr Denton?'

'That's right, Olive. Is there or isn't there?'

'No,' she said calmly. 'I'm alone. Have you seen the evening papers, Mr Denton?'

'I didn't have the time to read them. I guess they haven't said much that I don't know. Tell me, have the police been there since?'

'No, they haven't. Do you think they will be calling on me again?'

He laughed shortly. He said, 'It's hardly likely. And you haven't been in touch with them?'

'Now I know why you contacted me. You're worried.'

'Just a little. Wouldn't you be worried if you were in my shoes?'

'If I were in your shoes and as blameless as you say, I'd be inclined to tell my tale, Mr Denton. But I am not your mentor.'

'No, you're not, Olive. So you haven't talked?'

'I haven't talked. I guess it makes me a fool of some description. Or it could be the training I received in my childhood. My parents taught me how to grow up and mind my own business.'

'Smart parents, Olive. I — '

'Goodbye, Mr Denton.'

She hung up on him.

He felt miserable when she did so. There was something about her manner and her voice that was cool and steady and comforting. It was as though she really belonged to a more genteel age, an age when there was less fuss in the world, when the world had travelled less rapidly but got to where it was going just the same. He had never known such an age, merely heard of it and read of it. And yet he knew an odd nostalgia, as if he had accumulated the experiences of a century.

He must be going crazy.

He tried Claire's number again but got no answer. He tumbled into bed without undressing. The night was warm, clammy, and he unbuttoned his shirt front and lay on top of the covers. He stared at the dark ceiling, watching pictures there as he would have watched a TV or cinema screen. The pictures troubled him. They made no sense. After a while he dozed. The nightmare attained dimension and substance, and closed in on him.

He woke panting, his whole body running with sweat. He simply couldn't go on like this. Someone had taken him for a sucker and now he was being taken for a killer. Everything in him rebelled against being branded as a killer. But what could he do about it, short of going to the police and giving them the true story?

He had waited too long. If he went to them at this late stage and admitted what he had done, they would figure that his nerve had given up on him. They would think he was putting on an act to wriggle off the hot seat.

He had been dreaming of Claire Paige. In the nightmare Claire had been flaunting handfuls of money in front of his eyes. She had been laughing in that abandoned fashion which struck him as strange. She had been telling him he shouldn't have murdered Hank Otis and then he would have received his share of the money.

He twisted and turned in the darkness, trying to dispel the haunting edges of the dream.

He flung his feet to the floor finally. His throat was dry as dust and there was a ropey taste in his mouth. He would fix himself a drink and that might help him to sleep better.

He glanced at his wristwatch. The time was three a.m. By now Claire would be in bed, sleeping. Or would she be sleeping? He didn't have a monopoly on nightmares. She was bound to be feeling the strain. He wished he could make up his mind about Claire. He wished he didn't have all those doubts concerning her.

Instead of making for the bottle of Scotch he went into the kitchenette and brewed coffee. He poured a cup and took it with him to the telephone. He hesitated briefly before dialling Claire Paige's number.

A minute passed. Then a deep male voice hit his ear.

'Yes? What is it?'

215

Denton was too stunned to answer. The first thing that entered his head was that the police were visiting with Claire, late and all as it was. But the voice had sounded raspy, heavy with sleep.

He sat there, holding on to the receiver, hearing a blurring of noise in the earpiece.

'Who is it?' Claire's voice now. High and threaded through with brittle anxiety.

Denton didn't answer her. His stomach had gone into coils and the sweat on his brow was like ice water. He pulled himself together, replaced the telephone gently on its rest. An ache pounded through his head. He saw a vision of that tall man striding along the passage on Claire's floor to reach the elevator. It just had to be the tall man. Her companion. Her confederate. Her lover.

The heat went out of his thinking and he grew calm. He sat on by the phone for a few minutes, staring at the wall. Then he laid his coffee cup aside and went to get his shoes and coat.

Five minutes later he was on the street, walking in the dim lighting to his car. As

216

far as he could see there were no vehicles staked out in the area. The street was quiet at this hour. Aloft, the sky was a curtain of black velvet, sprinkled with restless stars.

Shutting himself in the Volkswagen, he began driving towards St Ann's Avenue.

He had the roads to himself, apart from the odd cab racing back to the depot. At an intersection he noticed a prowl car parked, and he slowed going past it. He watched in the driving mirror but the car didn't follow him. He made it to St Ann's Avenue and the Biltmore block in fifteen minutes from leaving Ethna Road.

There were a few vehicles squatting on the forecourt of the building. All of them were in darkness and apparently deserted. Denton swung away from the forecourt, moving over to the opposite side of the road to take advantage of the heavy shadows cast by the half-finished hulk of another building project.

Denton killed the Volkswagen's engine and switched off the lights. A weak light glimmered from the lobby of the apartment block, and even as he glanced

217

towards it he saw a shadowy figure emerge.

The figure was that of a man, a pretty tall man, wearing a soft hat snapped sharply across the pale blob that was his features. He stood in the thin glow coming from the lobby for a moment, looking about him. Satisfied that the coast was clear, he walked to a car. From this distance it was impossible to distinguish the car from the others parked nearby. A door slammed and the motor sprang to life. As the car moved on to the road Denton ducked his head. Should the stranger switch to full beam at this angle the headlamps would throw the Volkswagen out in relief.

The car straightened before the lights came on. A fierce pressure on the accelerator sent it leaping down the road. Denton raised his head to look. He had no doubt the stranger was at the wheel of the big shiny Oldsmobile.

Denton cursed softly. So his hunch had been right. Now he knew who had spoken to him on Claire's phone. He knew who had broken into the warehouse in front of him. He and Claire had laid an elaborate plan. His part in the plan had been that of sucker, fall guy. She had conned him into going after the money in the safe. If the gag had gone off as expected, the stranger would have socked him on the head — as he had done — would have left him for the cops to find after putting in an anonymous call. Likely he would have said he was passing the warehouse when he noticed something suspicious — a man prowling in the vicinity of the warehouse, a light behind the door.

The cops would have closed in on the building and he would have been picked up, and meanwhile the tall stranger would have been high-tailing with the twenty grand. Claire had played her cards well, worming her way into his confidence, making him fall in love with her. He would have been so conditioned that he would never have suspected Claire of involvement, never have mentioned her name to the police.

But the gag had slipped. Something

had stirred Hank Otis to go to the warehouse — a glimmering of suspicion, anxiety for the safety of the twenty thousand in his safe. He had surprised Claire's confederate. Hank must have brought his gun along for protection. There may have been a struggle. The stranger had wrested Hank's gun from him and shot him. He hadn't panicked either, which made him a cool cookie. He had stayed where he was until the time appointed for his — Denton's — arrival. He had stood behind the door and slugged him, thinking that the trick might still go off as planned. Afterwards, he had called the police and made his escape from the area.

Denton could scarcely believe that Claire was capable of such a scheme. But what had he really known of her prior to the five-dollar bait she had laid for him and her subsequent thaw? She had seemed a pillar of stability and respect to all who knew her at the mail order outfit, while underneath she was fretting and awaiting the opportunity to make a break with a few thousand dollars in her purse.

Denton shook his head as if to rid it of the sickening thoughts that plagued him. He was tempted to go up to Claire's apartment and have it out with her on the spot. She may have planned for robbery, but she certainly hadn't planned for murder. The right amount of pressure could have her squealing for mercy.

Maybe. Maybe not. Basically, she must be tough and ruthless, and he could find her laughing in his face, challenging him to do his worst and see if the police believed him.

What he should have done if he was anxious for action was followed the stranger to his hideout. But there would be another time. If he kept his nerve and played it cool he might beat the pair at their own game. If his phone call hadn't frightened the guy off permanently.

Denton drove back home and went to bed.

In the morning he felt less worried and harassed. Having plumbed Claire to her depths had given him a new strength and courage, a new resolve. Let the cops work at him if it made them happy. He hadn't murdered Hank Otis and his conscience was clear. Well, it wasn't as besmirched as it might have been.

The day commenced normally in the warehouse office. It was exactly like old times, except for the absence of Hank Otis. Jack Rhodes flitted in and out himself, detailing work to Claire, which she in turn detailed as she always did. Jimmy Florian seemed blithely cheerful. He had been questioned by the police also, but his private opinion was that the robbery had been an outside job. Tragedy had abounded yesterday, but today it ran off him as water runs off a duck. Occasionally he came into the office whistling. He stopped whistling when Claire gave him a chill, admonishing stare.

She was back in her deep-freeze with a vengeance. When it was necessary to speak to Denton she did so in a cool, impersonal voice and with her features schooled to neutrality. But he noticed she was pale and tense. She was worried and balanced on a fine edge. This gave him a certain sadistic satisfaction. He thought he would have hated her on sight after last night; he was amazed that he didn't. And yet it was impossible to say now what he did feel for her.

Lunch time came and he went to the diner on Pollard Street with Kirk Mason. Mason appeared to be excited about something.

'Have you seen how the Snow Queen is behaving this morning, Blake?'

'Miss Paige?' Denton frowned, wondering what smart notions Kirk was manufacturing on the side. 'I don't get it.'

'She's as frightened as sin,' Mason expanded with enthusiasm. 'Every time the office door opens she jumps a mile. Well, maybe just about a quarter mile.'

'So?' Denton urged tersely. 'She jumps when the door opens. So what? She hasn't gotten over the fact that Hank is dead. She feels lonesome because no one runs a hand over her any more. What else do you read into it?'

Mason started to answer him but paused, fork poised midway to his mouth. He had seen an intensity in Denton that threw him out of stride. He laughed drily.

'Forget it, Blake,' he said weakly.

'No, I won't forget it. Come on. I like a guy who gets flashes of inspiration. I find him interesting.'

'Aw, hell, it's nothing, Blake.'

'You're a curly-tailed liar, Kirk. It's something.'

'I just thought of the way she planted that money for you. Remember? The five-dollar bill. I said she might be leading you on.'

'Yeah, you did. So you told this to the cops?'

'I what? Are you nuts?' Mason began to redden. 'Of course I didn't. I was just thinking . . . '

'And what were you thinking?' Denton prodded. 'Why go bashful on an old pal?'

'Well, supposing — only supposing mind you — '

'Naturally. Get the hell on with it. What are you supposing? That the Snow Queen made off with the dough, shooting Hank in his breathing apparatus when he tried to stop her?'

'You'd say it's crazy, Blake. But is it so crazy? Who else had a key to the front door? Who else knew the combination of that safe in there?'

Denton felt a cold lump gathering in the pit of his stomach. He laughed derisively.

'Claire steal the dough? Kill old Hank? Please, Kirk, you must be able to do better than that.'

Mason had gone pale now and he grinned sheepishly.

'Well, it is an idea.'

'Try selling it to the cops,' Denton grunted. 'They'll love it.'

He was glad when the lunch break was over and he could get away from Mason. Still, it showed he had considered it, and therefore showed how the cops could consider it. Only the cops wouldn't think Claire had done it alone. They would smell collusion with a second party, and they might be working on the angle at this very minute.

With a jolt he remembered the stuff he had dumped over a hedge. He should have checked to see if it was still there.

14

She manoeuvred a trick to see him at five o'clock.

Immediately quitting time came, Denton covered his typewriter, left the office in front of Claire and headed for the street. Punctual as he was in leaving, Kirk and Sally Baines had left a few minutes earlier and were driving off in Mason's car as he cut across the parking area to reach the Volkswagen.

He heard feet hurrying over the asphalt after him and turned his head. Claire was bustling to overtake him.

'Oh, Mr Denton, I wonder if you could spare a moment. My car was acting strangely at lunch time.'

Not nearly as strangely as you've been acting all day, Denton thought grimly.

'I'll have a look at it.'

She had parked on the far fringe of the zone and where they wouldn't be visible from the street. He walked on before her,

226

halting when he reached her car.

'It seems to be the engine,' she said.

'Get inside and release the hood.'

She fumbled her keys from her purse and glanced over her shoulder to make sure they were not being observed.

'It was just an excuse, Blake . . . '

'Get inside and release the hood,' he said curtly. 'You might think we're in the clear, but I don't. There could be cops spying around.'

With a searching look at him, she did as he told her. The hood raised she came round to join him. He ducked his head and began fiddling with the distributor.

'Okay, Claire. What is it?'

'There's nothing really wrong, Blake. I just wanted — '

'I'm not talking about the motor,' he interrupted her. 'What else is bugging you?'

'Oh, Blake!' she groaned. 'Is it necessary to treat me as if I've got an infectious disease?'

He stared bleakly at her, saying nothing for a few seconds. She looked so harassed and vulnerable he had an urge to grab her into his arms. He smothered the urge, telling himself to wise up. Whatever private grief she was wallowing in, she had wished it on herself. She had two-timed him from the word go.

'What do you expect me to do, Claire? You laid it on the line last night. Perhaps you were right. In any case, I think it is a good idea to wrap it up and hope for the best.'

'I want to ask you something. Did-did you try and contact the apartment last night?'

So that was it? She wondered if he had caught on about her confederate and bed-mate. She had been in a stew since he made the phone call and was desperate for confirmation that he hadn't.

'Why should I have phoned you? We talked plenty. You made it plain which side of the fence you preferred.'

'Then you didn't ring? Someone did, Blake. It must have been around three.'

He frowned, pretending to be baffled.

'What did the guy say? What made you think it might have been me?'

'That's just it. Whoever it was didn't

say a thing. The phone burred. I answered it. But no one replied.'

'Somebody dialled the wrong number, I guess. Is this all you want to know?'

She hesitated, gnawing at her underlip. He saw a resolve commence fluttering in her eyes, but it went away as though she had stamped firmly on it. Her gaze hardened.

'I'm sorry, Blake.'

'Sure. So am I. You car is okay.' He lowered the hood and stood back, making a show of bringing a handkerchief from his pocket and wiping his hands, for the benefit of anyone who might be spying on them. 'See how it goes.'

She sat behind the wheel and looked at him, waiting for him to weaken, to make a gesture of understanding and compassion. At last she started the engine and drove towards the street. Her shoulders had lost their stiffness, become slack and rounded. As if the weight she was carrying was getting too much for her to bear.

Denton stared moodily until she went from his sight. Then he lit a cigarette and cut out for the Volkswagen.

He was about to hit Cable Street when he saw a convertible roll along from his left. The driver was a girl. As the car drew level with him he recognized her as Olive Overton. She didn't move her head on her way past, and so she didn't notice him.

Yielding to an impulse, Denton drove after her.

It was quite a distance down the street to the building where the girl lived. He slowed to give her time to take the car into the basement garage. When she emerged he was standing with his back to the wall, looking up and down the thoroughfare.

'Oh,' she said coolly. 'It's you again. Did you leave something when you were here last?'

Denton shook his head. He mustered a grin. She shrugged and went round the side of the building, entering a wide doorway giving access to the service elevator. They rode up together, looking at each other, not saying anything. She was wearing a white linen dress that set off the firm lines of her body. She was pretty without being beautiful, he decided. She wasn't just as luscious as Claire Paige, but she had a definite attractiveness that could easily grow on him.

They stepped out on the narrow hallway and continued to her attic apartment. She gave him a paper bag to hold while she took a key from her purse and opened the door. She cast a quick glance at him.

'The place could be crawling with police.'

'You're trying to frighten me. It isn't necessary. Just tell me to beat it and I'll go.'

She lifted her shoulders slightly, retrieved the paper bag from him, and entered the apartment. He followed her in and closed the door behind him.

'It's like a haven up here,' he said whimsically. 'You don't hear any traffic. You don't hear folks nattering at each other. I could go for a haven in the clouds.'

'I thought you had a pad all to yourself.'

'Oh, I do. But it isn't the same. It lacks — well, it could be atmosphere. What have you got in the bag — something to eat?'

She smiled faintly. It made the tip of her nose turn up.

'If I'd known you were coming . . . '

'Sure, sure. You'd have baked a cake. I saw you drive past in your car. I was taken with a sudden irrational impulse to follow you.'

'Because you don't trust me?'

'I trust you all right. That's what gets me somewhat. Your simple faith in human nature. Your willingness to take life as it comes to you.'

'It could be apathy, Mr Denton. That would shake your romantic notions to the roots?'

'I guess it would,' he said musingly. 'But it isn't so. You intrigue me and that has got to mean something. Look, I'm talking like the centre pages of a book on psychic phenomena. Do you mind if I stay and have a cup of coffee with you?'

'Of course not. Let's go into the galley. You can sit and be a witty conversationalist. Or you can be silent if you want and meditate. If you're hungry you can stir a pan of instant potato.'

They worked together on a meal as if they had been doing it every day for the past year. The meal ready, they sat down in the kitchen to eat it. If she was anxious to hear what developments had taken place since he was here last she gave no indication of the fact.

'How is the art work coming along?' he asked presently.

'Fair enough. I can't complain. I'll never make a fortune out of it, but if it keeps me eating why should I grumble?'

'And you're happy?'

She thought about it for a minute, raised one shoulder in a careless motion.

'What is happy? Having money? Maybe. Don't ask me, Mr Denton.'

'Blake.'

'You didn't kill that man, Blake?'

'Of course I didn't. He was dead when I arrived at the office. The killer slugged me. Etcetera, etcetera. I told you before. I was taken for a sucker.'

'By your girl?'

He looked steadily at her.

'She isn't my girl. Well, I did have a

crush on her. It was the way she planned it.'

'She and some other man?'

'Here!' He laughed harshly. 'You've been thinking about it, trying to work it out. It really isn't any of your business, Olive. The less you know of it the better. The cops figure me as their prime suspect. They're breathing against my neck.'

'So?' Her slim, capable fingers toyed with her coffee cup. 'You realize what you must do, Blake. It's the only sensible thing to do.'

'Give myself up? Yeah, I have thought of it. Plenty. But what would it get me? I'll tell you. They'd say I'm telling only part of the story. They'd say I was picking the easy way out because I'm scared.'

'You aren't scared?'

He looked at her. He wondered why he was confiding in her, why it was so easy to talk to her and confide in her. It was like the last time he'd been here. There was something about her that drew him out and drew him towards her. He sighed.

'Yes, I am scared. I'd be a fool if I

wasn't scared. I was a fool to fall for the idea in the first place. Tell me, Olive, you aren't married?'

She laughed as though he'd just made a hilarious joke. At the same time twin spots of colour stained her cheeks. Her laughter caused Denton to feel confused.

'All right. Let it ride. I've no business prying into your personal life.'

'But I'm not married,' she said, sobering. 'I was engaged once to a nice boy, but we didn't get along and we broke it off. That satisfy your curiosity?'

'I'm sorry.'

'Because I'm not married? I don't see — '

'Oh, drop it, Olive,' he broke in. 'Not because you haven't married. Because I'm breaking the rules of etiquette.'

She shrugged the idea off. She poured more coffee for him. She accepted the cigarette he offered her. They continued talking. She gave him a sketchy outline of her history. Denton reciprocated. Time passed. He asked himself what was happening to him, if he was right in the head. She was like an oasis, and he a thirsty traveller who wanted to linger by her. If only he hadn't been so stupid as to tie in with Claire . . .

★ ★ ★

She went straight home to her apartment in St Ann's Avenue. She closed the door on herself, put her back to it, and cried, giving free rein to the emotion that stormed in her.

Since leaving Blake Denton she had been hard put to hold herself together. She was a fool to have taken Blake into the plan, a fool for having listened to Jim Case in the first place.

But Case had always been able to wind her about his little finger. He was like a poison that she had to have, even though she realized too much of him could make a fatal dose.

Jim Case had always fascinated her.

Four years ago, when he'd been a stickman at the Las Vegas club where she'd gone to work as a hostess, he had pinned her down with one devouring glance from his dark eyes. Case was tall, strongly-built, and with an animal vitality and magnetism it was impossible to resist. Even then she could read the potential in the man, for menace, savagery; even for stark tragedy. She had disregarded the warnings of her common sense. Case was like a strong, heady drink that she must taste, must sample.

She had tasted. She had thrilled to the devil's brew he represented. Within a week she was going out with Case; within ten days she was his mistress. He'd told her how he admired her resistance.

They lived and worked together in Vegas for a year. Case seemed a careful man: a careful drinker and careful person with his money. He said had had some money stashed by. He was saving, and now that he had met Claire he would save all the harder. One day, when he had the right amount in the kitty, he would break with the gambling circuit, move over into California. He liked California, he said. He liked living on the coast. He would start his own club. Claire would help him run it.

Then the blow came.

One night two toughs had called at their chalet quarters near the woods. Case was a big man, but these two men were bigger still. They were tough and merciless, and Claire knew enough about the business to realize why they were there.

They took Case away. He knew he was beaten and that fighting would be useless. When they dropped him at the front door an hour later he was battered half to death.

But he survived. When he was able to talk the story came out. He had been working the layout he operated to his own advantage, milking a steady thousand dollars a week. The bosses had discovered his deceit. The toughs were the weapons they used. They could have killed Case, but they let him live. But there was one condition in the mercy contract. He had a week in which to get over the state line. If he refused to obey the order — or ever came back — he would be killed within the space of twenty-four hours.

Fully recovered, he took Claire to California with him. They moved around a lot, picked up what work they could. Then, as suddenly as Jim Case had come into Claire's life, he'd vanished.

She spent some time pining for him, searching for him. The months passed and she never found him. She concluded he had gone off with another woman.

She gave up working the night clubs, took a secretarial course, and finally landed a steady office job. Two years ago she had come to Maxwell and secured a decent job with *Advance Mail Order*. She had practically forgotten Jim Case until a month ago, when she ran into him in a downtown store.

He apologized for running out on her. His reason was that the Las Vegas bosses had changed their minds about him and were coming after him to rub him out. He had not wanted to frighten her, and so he had vanished without making an explanation.

Of course she knew he was telling her lies. He was a liar and a cheat and he would always be so. But she couldn't find it in her to reject him. Immediately his hand touched her she had tingled with anticipation. She had fought against the sensation, telling herself he was no good for her and would never be any good for her. She had put her old way of life behind her and it would be a mistake to go back on her tracks.

But Case had a way of wiping out her worry.

She had brought him home and he had talked. At the moment his fortunes were at a low ebb, but there was something promising in the pipeline if he could get his hands on a little capital to take it off the ground. There was no future for her slaving in a dingy office, was there? With the right slice of luck they could make the strike they had dreamed of. It wouldn't take the earth to swing it, Case explained, just ten thousand dollars or so.

It was the instant when Claire thought of the deal Hank Otis was making with the salesman, Probart. She had told Denton that the salesman was called Waterman and he traded in stolen or smuggled watches. But she had done it in order to salve Blake's conscience if it troubled him. He would reason how it was no great sin to rob a trickster of his ill-gotten gains.

After telling Jim Case all about the twenty thousand which would soon be locked in Otis' ancient safe, and how she carried a front door key and knew the safe's combination, he had taken over the planning with enthusiasm. It was his idea to enlist the aid of someone who would serve as a fall guy for the robbery. Claire gave him all the details and he took it from there, schooling her as to how she should set about conditioning Denton.

At first she had refused to involve another party, but Case had talked her into it. Besides Otis and Rhodes, she was the only one who carried a door key and knew the combination of the safe. If she didn't agree to the precaution he suggested she would find herself being accused of the robbery. From there the police might commence investigating her former background and come up with the information that she had been a Vegas night club hostess. Was she prepared to run this risk?

Eventually she succumbed to Case's

persuasion. It was another illustration of the way the crook could manipulate her. Denton would go to steal the money at around two o'clock; Case would use the key Claire gave him and be in the office when Denton arrived. He would slug him on the head, not too hard, but hard enough to keep him under for the time it would take Case to get the money out of the building and for the police to descend on the warehouse in response to his anonymous alarm call.

Of course the money would not be found with Denton, but he would be on a spot all the same and be branded as the thief. Later the police might think of a confederate who had fought with Denton in the office, knocked him unconscious and made off with the twenty thousand. Whatever happened, Denton would not involve Claire, never suspecting how she had used him for her own ends. Later still when the fuss had died down, Case and Claire would leave Maxwell and start a new life together.

But Hank Otis had come to his office that night. He had surprised Case, and

Case had shot him with his own gun. That was called murder, a crime which Claire had not bargained for. And now she was sure Blake Denton suspected something. She felt a trap closing in on her. She did not trust Case.

When the telephone rang she cried out with the shock it gave her.

15

A detective awaited Denton when he reached home.

He was leaning against the wall as Denton entered the passage and he straightened on his approach and looked business-like.

'Blake Denton?'

'That's right.' The warm glow that had been generated back in Olive Overton's place vanished. Denton's eyes narrowed on the other. He was flashing a badge.

'Detective Officer Washburn, Denton. You're wanted down at Headquarters.'

'Oh.' Denton glanced up and down the passage. Washburn misinterpreted this and stepped closer to him.

'Don't try any tricks, Denton. I've got a gun here. Start running out on me and I'll have to shoot.'

Anger began biting at Denton.

'Give me thirty minutes,' he said. 'I've just got home. I want to wash, change my shirt . . . '

'Look, pal, quit stalling, will you. Are you going to come quietly or do you want to make a fuss?'

Denton shrugged and preceded the detective to the top of the stairway.

Down on the street an official car swept forward. It had been lying back out of range until the driver saw Washburn emerge. The detective waited until Denton got in and then slid on to the seat beside him.

'Get going, Frank.'

The car gouged into the traffic flow, disregarding the sudden blaring of horns. The driver stuck his head out of the window and glared at a big truck driver who had been making the most noise. The truck driver coloured and glared at the automobile pressing on his tail. Frank chuckled and looked smug. He drove fast but with great skill.

Denton paid no heed to what was going on. He was still stunned by the arrival of the detective. He was trying to work out what developments had taken place in the Otis killing. Had the police discovered fresh evidence — evidence that made him a positive link with the crime? He shuddered and came out in a cold sweat.

Washburn watched him from the corner of his eye.

'What's the matter, Denton?' he said with a tight smile. 'Getting the wind up?'

'I've no reason to get the wind up,' Denton retorted flatly. 'But hell, I guess I have. Once you guys get an idea in your heads you won't let it go.'

'Or a clue,' Washburn said.

'A clue? What kind of clue? What do you mean? I didn't murder Hank Otis . . .'

The detective motioned him to silence.

'Well, I don't know,' he admitted. 'I was ordered to pick you up and I've picked you up.'

Denton had stayed longer at Olive Overton's place than he'd intended. Daylight was fading from the sky and already street lamps were being turned on. How long had Washburn been waiting for him? Had the police spotted his car parked at the far end of Cable Street? Had they pressured Claire to the point where she'd talked? This didn't seem likely. Claire was too smart to talk. If she did talk she would make certain no blame would be laid at her feet.

Finally they cruised to a halt opposite the building housing Police Headquarters. Peering through the car window at it, a hard knot gathered in Denton's stomach. His legs were so weak they would scarcely take his weight when he alighted. Washburn urged him into a long, dimly-lit corridor in front of him. They climbed a short flight of stairs and halted at a door. The detective rapped and opened the door.

He said, 'Here is Denton, Lieutenant.'

'What the hell kept you?' Granger said waspishly.

'He wasn't at home when I called. I had to wait for him.'

'Okay,' Granger grunted. 'That's all for now. Tell Wirrel to stand by, will you.'

Washburn went out and closed the door on the lieutenant and Denton. Denton found himself in a small room with a desk and three chairs. Granger sat behind the desk on one of the chairs, a fat cigar jutting from the corner of his mouth. Another of the chairs was over by the opposite wall. The third was placed in front of the desk. Granger nodded at Denton to be seated.

Denton sat down. He ran his tongue across his lips.

'I'd like to know what this is all about, Lieutenant.'

His voice was hoarse and not too steady. Granger noticed and his gaze became bleak. He pointed at some stuff on the desk top and Denton's blood froze in his veins.

Granger said nothing for a moment; neither did Denton. From the reserves of his nerve and courage he grabbed desperately at what was available. His features registered puzzlement and then blankness. He made a slight shrugging motion with his shoulders. 'I don't get it.'

Granger dragged his eyes from him. He lifted a bedraggled rubber glove, held it aloft briefly and dropped it. He lifted another rubber glove and did the same thing with it. Next he lifted a key and held it for Denton to look at. He said nothing. He stopped and brought a small bundle of polythene from the floor at his feet. This he dropped on the desk. He stooped again and produced a short-handled shovel. He let it clatter down on top of the desk. Traces of dirt adhered to the blade of the shovel.

Granger looked at Denton.

'Well, mister, what have you got to say about it?'

Denton's laugh was the sound of a creaky door being swung on its hinges.

'Say about what? That junk? Did you ever try taking a rabbit out of a hat, Lieutenant?'

For an instant Granger's face looked murderous. He got himself under control. His cigar had gone out and he lit it from a folder of paper matches.

'You've seen this junk before?' he said.

'Never. What does it mean?'

Granger studied him for a long time, sitting and puffing at his cigar whilst his gaze remained fixedly on Denton.

'I'll tell you. It was found on a plot of waste ground, Denton. A place where kids play. It was a bunch of kids who found it today. We might never have heard of it, but one of the kids is the son of a police officer. The kid showed the key and the shovel to his dad — By the way, Denton, we never fingerprinted you did we?'

'No, you didn't,' Denton said thickly. He was sunk. His prints would be all over the shovel and the key. All they had to do was print him and match the results with those on the key and shovel. But wait a minute! Granger was bluffing him. He hadn't found his prints on the stuff. Kids had been playing with it. The shovel was dirty and showed it had been used. His own prints would be smudged to hell and yonder. And what could they lift from the key? This was just a gag to get him to walk into a trap. Granger expected him to break down and confess. Had he managed to get a good set of prints from any of the items he wouldn't have been so keen on flashing them. He would have had them matched with his own, and by now the case he was attempting to make against him would be sealed and delivered. Also, he was pretty certain that the finger-print men had been busy at the *Advance* office. They could get a dozen good sets from the things he handled daily on his desk.

'Have you any objections to being printed?'

Denton shook his head. If it was a bluff then he was ready to call it.

'I don't understand, though.'

'What don't you understand?' Granger probed gently.

'What that stuff has got to do with me — or you either, Lieutenant.'

Granger's eyes drilled into him.

Watching him, Denton knew he had him beaten. They had lifted his prints. They had examined the articles for prints. But they hadn't been able to find anything to match.

Granger lifted the key.

'This opens the front door of the warehouse where you work. But it isn't a legitimate key. What I mean is, Rhodes claims it is a new key. It is a new key. It was cut by using one of the original keys as a copy.'

Denton made a stab in the dark.

251

'If you know all that it must narrow down the field. All you have to do is find out where it was cut and ask the guy there to say who ordered it.'

Granger's gaze lowered fractionally. For a lieutenant of detectives he couldn't drill his feelings too well. Denton was able to follow his thoughts as though they were printed in an open book.

'Easier said than done,' Granger admitted. 'It doesn't have the manufacturer's stamp. There are three places in Maxwell where you can have keys cut. None of them remembers cutting this one, but they confess they could have cut it.'

'Oh.'

'You sound relieved, mister. You sound as though you known damn well we can't trace whoever cut it. You're a pretty smart guy, Denton. You've been around. You know scores. I've told you how kids discovered this stuff, so you know it was handled. You know we've got your prints, but they don't tally with what we were able to lift. That puts us up a pole — you think.'

'But — '

Granger waved him to silence. He lifted the phone on his desk and dialled. He had an immediate answer.

'Hello, Mr Keller. Yeah, this is Lieutenant Granger again. Sorry for keeping you so long. Could we visit at your place now, do you think? We could? Swell! Yeah, we're starting out at once.'

Granger hung up, rose and lifted his hat from a peg on the wall. Denton stared blankly at him.'

'Can I go?'

'You're coming with me, Denton. We're going to see a guy that runs a gardening store here in town.'

Denton felt a wave of utter dismay. He tried to force a laugh.

'A gardening store? What's with a gardening store? Why do you want me with you?'

Granger came round the desk and towered over him.

'I'll tell you, chum. If you need to be told, that is. Whoever broke into the joint where you work knew the money was in Hank Otis' safe. Right?'

'Sure. But . . . '

'One thing at a time, Denton. The guy who did it was smart. Like you are smart. He had planned the grab to the last detail. When he snatched the twenty grand from the safe he didn't intend bringing it home with him. That would have been stupid, would it not? His home would have been searched eventually — providing he was an obvious suspect. Which you are, friend, believe it or not. So what does the guy do? You can't make a guess? I'll tell you. He bought a shovel and piece of plastic. So now a pattern emerges. The duplicate key to open the door. The sheet of plastic to wrap the dough in. Don't ask me why the guy was going to wrap the dough. I'll tell you. He intended hiding it somewhere until the heat died. Where better to hide it than in a hole in the ground? Which brings on the shovel. You can surely work out why he needed a pair of rubber gloves. But two pairs? Well, I don't know. In case he had an accident with the first pair and ripped them?'

'But — '

'Come on, Denton. Keller is waiting for us. He identified the shovel as one from his stock. I want him to have a gander at you and see if we can jolt his memory.'

Denton stood up. His legs felt so rubbery beneath him he was certain they wouldn't carry him to the door. Granger gave his shoulder a push.

'Just a minute, Lieutenant . . . '

'Yeah?' Triumph glinted in the detective's eyes. 'You want to call it off and save everybody a pile of trouble?'

'Are you crazy?' Denton said huskily. 'But the money. It *was* stolen from the office safe, wasn't it?'

Granger's brows furrowed darkly.

'Sure it was. And buried, likely. There was plenty of dirt on the shovel, but it all came from that vacant lot. You must have cleaned it before the kids found it, Denton. Enough of the mouth-flapping and head for the street.'

The car that had brought Denton to the building was parked with the driver still at the wheel. The detective called Washburn bustled out behind them. Granger spoke to Washburn.

'You frisked him all right?'

'What!' Washburn began to redden. 'I didn't think — '

'Period,' Granger rapped tersely. 'Do it.'

Denton was submitted to the indignity of having to spread his arms on the roof of the car while the detective patted him expertly.

'He's clean.'

'What did you expect?' Denton said fiercely. A couple of bystanders had halted to stare at them.

'Shut up, punk,' Granger said. 'Get into the car.'

The lieutenant got in with the driver while Washburn got in back with Denton. The smug driver started the engine running and lunged out from the curb.

It had been a trick to humiliate him, Denton realized when he had cooled off. They hadn't expected to find him armed with a gun or any other weapon. It was some of Granger's subtle psychology to break up his defences and make him feel small and guilty. A little more of the same treatment and he would be soft enough to crumple.

He just thought, Denton reflected grimly.

His spirits kept on dropping all the same as the car nosed nearer to the market quarter where he had purchased the shovel, polythene and rubber gloves. He remembered the old guy who had sold him the items. He had worn thick-lensed glasses and seemed half blind. He hoped his memory was as poor as his eyesight.

The centre was in darkness except for the store with the name Keller in green neon tubing above the window. Granger and Washburn alighted, Granger telling the driver to stay where he was.

'Let's go, Denton,' he said gruffly.

They walked to the big glass door and the lieutenant pressed on the bell push. A few seconds later the door swung open and the old guy Denton remembered gestured them inside. He had a nervous air about him which raised Denton's hopes a trifle. A man who was nervous couldn't be very sure of himself.

Keller wanted to take them into his office at the rear.

'It's okay, Mr Keller,' Granger told him. 'This will do fine. Put on the rest of your lights, will you?'

Keller hurried to a switchboard and triggered the switches. The showroom became flooded with white blinding light.

'Step forward, Denton.'

Denton took a slow step towards the storekeeper. The way the lights glinted on Keller's thick lenses dazzled him. He blinked a couple of times. Keller looked at him for several seconds and spoke.

'Well, I — uh — It's hard to say, Lieutenant. I do a good line in those shovels. It's the time of year when everybody's buying gardening stuff . . . '

'Plastic sheeting?' Granger said curtly. 'Rubber gloves?'

Keller cackled inanely. His eyes were like great glass marbles behind his glasses. They stayed rivetted on Denton.

'Sure, sure,' he said nervously. 'I sell that kind of thing every day. I must have sold six pairs of rubber gloves today. I sold plenty of plastic. They make frames, you see.'

'Look, Mr Keller,' Denton said steadily,

'don't let these cops rush you into saying what you don't want to say. Now tell them the truth. You remember me or you don't?'

'Lay off,' Washburn said harshly. 'Keep your mouth shut, Denton.'

'No, he's right, he's right. I'm not going to turn a man in for the hell of it . . . ' Keller went on studying Denton. He pulled a handkerchief from his hip pocket and mopped his brow. He shrugged his stooped shoulders, shook his head.

'Well?' Granger said thinly.

'I'm sorry, Lieutenant.'

'You don't remember him?'

'No, I must admit I don't. It's not to say he didn't buy things from me within the past day or so, but I get so many strangers I can't be sure.'

Granger's breath ran out in a ragged sigh. He turned to the door.

'Thanks, anyhow, Mr Keller. Okay, everybody, out.'

Denton shuddered in the shadows of the street. He was pushed into the rear seat of the car again and Washburn slammed down beside him. Granger resumed his seat in the front and told the driver to get going.

'Where to, Lieutenant — headquarters?'

Granger's hesitation was brief.

'No,' he said. 'Drop Denton off in Ethna Road first.'

Denton was silent on the journey. From time to time Washburn glanced at him, but he said nothing. They drove into Ethna Road and halted opposite Denton's apartment house. Washburn let him out.

'Be seeing you, pal.'

The door slammed and the car moved off. It took Granger back to headquarters. He went into his office and lit a cigar. He prowled about the room for a while. A few minutes later he called in Ed Raven from the detectives room.

'Ed,' he said, 'there is one more angle I want to investigate. This Claire Paige dame. There is something about her. Dig into her past and don't stop digging until you get me a clue.'

16

Stifling her anxiety, Claire picked up the receiver.

'Yes? Who is it?'

'Who are you expecting?' Jim Case said with his mirthless laugh. 'Well, sweetie-pie, did you see him? Did you talk to him? How did it go?'

'I don't know, Jim,' the girl answered slowly.

'You don't know!' Case echoed. 'What do you mean, you don't know? You did talk to him?'

'Yes, yes, I did. But only for a few minutes . . .'

'Did you ask him if he had buzzed you at three o'clock this morning?' Case's voice had taken on a rough edge that rasped on Claire's nerves. She bit her underlip.

'Of course I did. He said he hadn't. But Jim . . .'

'Yeah?' he urged tautly. 'You don't believe him?'

'I'm not sure. He seems — But look, I'd better say nothing more until I see you.'

'When?' Case came back swiftly. 'I could drive over there now, sweetie, or do you want I should wait until dark?'

'No, Jim, don't come here. I've got a feeling it could be dangerous. For all I know I could really be under surveillance. I kidded Blake along that I was. But I could be, too.'

'Then come to my place,' Case said. 'Wait until it's dark and then make sure you aren't being tailed. Got it, Claire?'

'I wonder if it would be wise. Maybe we ought to stay away from each other for a few days, and — '

'Nothing doing, Claire. I mean it. I'm in this too, remember. Right up to my ears. I've got an idea. Don't use your own car. Get a cab.'

'Yes. All right, Jim. I'll see you about eight o'clock.'

'Don't disappoint me, sweetie-pie, will you. And pull yourself together. What the hell has come over you lately?'

'Nothing, Jim, nothing. I'm okay. I'm fine.'

Good,' he said. 'Good. It would be a pity if you went soft at this stage, honey. See you.'

He hung up.

Claire went into the kitchenette with the intention of putting a meal together. But she wasn't hungry and settled for a cup of coffee. There was a feeling growing in her that she could scarcely understand, much less fight against. It was a mixture of regret and fear, she deduced; but she couldn't be sure. Yet she was frightened; there was no doubt of that. And she did regret with all her heart having dragged Blake Denton into the deal.

She waited for Blake to call her on the phone or actually come visiting. But he wouldn't call and he wouldn't visit. Blake smelled a rat and at this very minute might be doing something definite about his suspicions. She shivered at the memory of Denton's grim features. He wasn't the fool they had taken him for. She had warned Case, but he had paid no heed to her warning. That was one of

Case's weakest points — he figured himself smarter than anyone else.

By eight it was full dark and she went down to the street. She stood for some minutes in the shadows beyond the lobby and looked carefully at the cars parked in the area. Her fears allayed somewhat, she walked briskly to her own car and a moment later was driving out of the avenue.

Although Case had told her to use a taxi cab she didn't want to bring a cab to the apartment building. She would do as she had done when meeting Denton and leave her car on a movie house lot, taking a cab from there.

She drove to the Galaxy on Moorhead Street, parked and circled the area to gain the opposite side of the street. She walked quickly to the end of the street, hailed a cab, and told the driver to take her to Tunley Avenue. Case's temporary address wasn't exactly Skid-row, but it wasn't far removed from it, either.

She asked to be let down at the corner of the street and walked from there to a cheap apartment building. She had almost reached the building when a car came along and slowed, edging to the curb. She froze in terror when the door was flung open and a smooth voice snaked to her ears.

'Coming for a ride, honey?'

At first she had thought it was police, but now she saw the white flash of teeth and anger boiled in her.

'Go pester somebody else, you bastards.'

A tinny laugh trickled to her. The car door slammed and the vehicle drew into the roadway and gathered speed. Claire trembled. She raced the remainder of the way to the dim hall where a flight of stairs led up to Jim Case's apartment.

The door opened on her first knock and she flung herself into the big man's arms.

He held her tightly for a moment, then pushed her from him to peer into her face. It was gathered in a tense, white mask in which her lips were two moist streaks.

'What happened?' he demanded roughly. 'Claire, don't tell me you allowed yourself to be followed here.'

'No, I didn't, Jim. A kerb-crawler scared the wits out of me. He came out of nowhere and I thought for a minute it was the police.'

'Slimy jerk,' Case rasped. 'If I had him by the neck he wouldn't do any crawling for a day or so. I know what you need right now, baby,' he went on with a faint grin. He pressed her to a chair in the small, shabby living room and brought a bottle of whisky from a sideboy. His back turned to her she couldn't see the dark frown that knotted his brow momentarily. He was six-feet two inches, wide in the shoulders, and with a swarthy, handsome face. He was dressed flashily as always, believing that no matter how far you dropped in the world it was important to dress nattily and drive a good car. 'Here, knock this back,' he said, handing Claire a glass that was three-quarters full. 'Then tell me what the beef is with Denton.'

She drank and told him, explaining how she had begun to freeze Denton out as he had instructed her to. But he hadn't taken it as she had meant him to take it.

'I thought I had him on a hook, Jim. I was sure it wouldn't take much to have him proposing marriage to me. But he isn't a fool. He doesn't just think that I'm scared for myself. He suspects there is more behind it. I'm certain he suspects that I deliberately rail-roaded him into a fix.'

'No kidding,' Case mused. He was seated opposite Claire, his thick thighs apart, holding his own glass of whisky between them. He was doing his best to keep the apprehension he felt from showing. 'But he wouldn't squeal to the cops, would he? He wouldn't be so dumb, honey. No matter how he jumps he lands in the centre of the fire. The only sensible course he has is to sit tight with his mouth shut and see if he can weather the storm.'

Claire nodded. She finished the whisky in her glass. The warm glow had reached her stomach and already she was recovering some of her nerve.

'You would think he would do that. But I don't know, Jim. I'm not sure. He's been around and he's the sort of person who wouldn't lie down and be tramped on.'

'What you're saying is he might start sniffing. If he did and realized you'd given him a raw deal he might get tough.'

'It's possible, Jim, and we can't afford to overlook the possibility.'

'Sure, sweetie, sure.' Case drained his glass and lit a cigarette. He seemed to be working something over in his mind.

'If only you hadn't shot Mr Otis, Jim.'

Colour crept into the big man's face and made it ugly.

'Don't give me that again,' he snapped angrily. 'How was I to know the old goat would turn up. He had a gun, hadn't he? He could have shot me with it. It was him or me, Claire, and you'd better see it my way.'

'I — I understand, Jim,' she said with a weak smile. 'But — but I've been thinking . . . You've got the money. You've got it hidden in the woods. It's what you wanted after all, a stake, something to get off the ground again. Well, you've got it. Take it, Jim. I don't want any of it. I can get by without it. Take it and leave town at once. Leave things as they are. The longer you stay here the more dangerous it's going to become for both of us. I — '

She stopped speaking at the expression in his eyes. He started to laugh but the laugh turned into a sneer instead.

'Cut out from you, baby! After I've found you again? Are you nuts? I figured I could get you out of my system, Claire, but I never did. Oh, no, Claire honey! Nothing doing. When I leave this burg you're going to come with me. We're together again and we're going to stay together. Here! Are you saying you don't love me any more? Because if you do I'm going to call you a pink-faced liar.'

Claire shuddered and dropped her eyes from him.

'Yes, yes, I do love you, Jim. But I can't run away at once. If I did the police would smell a rat and come after us. Don't you see,' she said, raising her eyes to meet his squarely, 'I'm going to have to sweat it out. For weeks. For months. In the meantime Denton could — '

'Forget Denton,' Case growled brusquely. He placed his glass on the floor and stood up. 'I know you're going to have to sweat it out until the heat dies, but I'll be here to sweat it out with you, sweetie. What's a matter of weeks, a matter of months? We've got twenty thousand bucks to compensate us for the strain.'

'But Denton, Jim . . . '

'I told you to forget him. He's just one guy. He's just human like the rest of us. Are you going to tell me the jerk is superhuman?'

The manner in which he said it struck a chill dread in Claire. Case didn't notice. He took her glass from her fingers, put it to one side. Then he gathered Claire into his arms and his mouth closed demandingly on hers.

When Case kissed her like this Claire was unable to think of anything but the raw ecstasy he sent coursing through her.

★ ★ ★

Denton twisted and turned in the darkness, trying to get to sleep. No matter how he tried he couldn't wipe the events of the evening from his mind. First the wonderful soothing interlude with Olive Overton, and then the merciless thrusting back into harsh reality. Granger suspected him of the robbery and the killing. There was no doubt of it. Tonight had proved it. And if Keller had been blessed with better eye-sight or a better memory he would be behind prison bars at this minute.

Where to go from here? He didn't know. But yes, he did. There was only one direction to follow and to stay pointing into until he had revealed Claire Paige for what she was — a schemer without feeling or scruples. The tag of Snow Queen suited her to a T. She was hard, cold, and unyielding, no matter what she had tried to impress on him to the contrary. But the woman was only part of it. The rest of the iceberg was hidden underneath. Her confederate. Her lover. The tall man. Who was he and where had she met him?

He drifted off to sleep finally, surrendering to the nightmare that inevitably awaited him.

He had no idea how long he had been

sleeping when something registered on the fringes of his consciousness and brought him awake.

He lay, staring into the blackness, not moving, straining his befogged senses to come to the alert.

The shadow came at him so suddenly it took him by surprise. At first it had been nothing more than a blob against the general darkness, but then it gained dimension and took on movement — murderous lunging movement.

He flung himself sideways at the last instant, hearing the whisper of air and glimpsing a shaft of thin light. The knife was plunged into the mattress still warm with his blood. With a desperate roll he landed on the floor, bounding upright in a smooth uninterrupted flow of movement.

The shadow came at him and he slugged wildly at a vaguely defined stomach area. The guy was fast as a snake. He rode the brunt of the blow and slammed his fist at the side of Denton's neck. It connected and sent him scattering, senses slithering back to the brink of oblivion.

By the time Denton reached his feet again the bedroom door was opening. Feet pounded through the apartment to the front door. Denton went after him, tripping in his haste. He heard the front door open and slam. He reached the door and snatched it open. The passage beyond was empty and feet were racketting down the stairs to the street. Denton went on to the street and was in time to see the tail-end of a car diminishing in the gloom.

He stood and sucked air into his lungs. He considered rushing to his own car and taking out after his assailant, undressed and all he was. But he didn't have the keys down with him, and even now the car was swinging round the corner of the street, tyres screaming at the treatment they were getting.

Denton jerked when another car across the way went into action. It did so suddenly and with fierce, surprising acceleration. It was zooming down the road in the wake of the other vehicle before Denton could collect his wits. Headlamps came on and bannered wide yellow swathes in front of it. The car seemed to take the corner on two wheels. It went from sight. The night calmed, went silent. The silence was shredded by a plane crashing through the sky overhead. Then silence came again. Denton went back upstairs, switched on the light.

He stood by his bed and looked at the knife sticking into the mattress. It had been jammed there with plenty of strength, plenty of feeling behind it. Murder feeling. Denton repressed a shiver. The guy who had done it was fit for a lot, fit to kill.

Fit to kill . . . He had killed Hank Otis. Denton was sure it was the same character. It didn't need a genius to see how the pattern was shaping. He was supposed to have fallen for the Otis slaying and the robbery. But he had wriggled off the spot, just made it and nothing more. It was where their plan had slipped: the plan cooked up by Claire Paige and the tall guy who had been visiting her. They were afraid of him going mushy and shooting off his mouth to the cops. They figured he was trying to reach a decision about this. They didn't want him to reach a decision. They wanted him dead, silently dead. Then the cops would think that he and his partner in the crime had fought and his partner had killed him.

Denton sweated. His whole body seemed to be enveloped in a coating of chill moisture. He drew the knife out and looked at it. Eight inches or so of cold steel. He found his cigarettes, lit one and sat down on the edge of the bed. His nerves wanted to go on shivering but he wouldn't let them. It was a tight right enough. Of course it was a tight. But he had been in them before. He had survived.

His thoughts swung to the second car in the street. Whose car had it been — Claire's? Yes, that could be it. She had come along for the ride and a grandstand view of the proceedings. He couldn't believe she could be so ruthless.

It might not have been Claire's car at all.

He went over to the phone and dialled her number. A minute passed by and then she answered.

'Yes?' Her voice was dull and heavy, loaded with anxiety. 'What is it?'

'It's me, Claire.'

'You! Blake . . . What is it, Blake? Is anything wrong?' Her voice soared and went on soaring.

'Yeah, there is,' he said bleakly. 'Do you know something baby, I'm really surprised at you. Real disappointed in you.'

'What are you talking about, Blake? What are you driving at?'

'You don't know?' he demanded tautly.

'I swear to heaven that I don't. Tell me!'

'You're a liar, Claire. But that doesn't matter much now. I just want to give you a thought to sleep on, liar. He didn't make it. He tried hard enough but it didn't come off. Now you give him a message from me, baby. It's a game that two can play at. Tell him so when you see him. Tell him I'm going to get him.'

He said nothing more. He heard her sharp gasp and then a muffled groan. But she didn't speak. She just went on listening as he was listening.

He smashed the receiver down hard on its hook.

Detective 2nd grade Cargill clumped back to the patrol car parked in the shadows of Tunley Avenue. He dropped down on the front seat beside the driver and lifted the radio mike.

'Car eight-three to Headquarters . . . '

'Come in eighty-three.'

'This is Joe, Sergeant. We followed the guy the whole of the way. He went to roost in Tunley Avenue. Number One, one, five. Apartment house. What do we do now?'

'Did you get a look at the car he was driving, check with the licence tag?'

'It wasn't possible. He ran the car into a garage at the rear. It's lock-up. We could bust it easily . . . '

'No, don't do it, Joe. It means he's living there. It means we can check out the details later.'

'Whatever you say, Sarge. We could stick around.'

'It isn't necessary. I tell you I'll have another check run on him. Call it off and come in. At least you can give me a reasonable description of the guy. Every little helps.'

Ed Raven signed off. Cargill replaced the mike, nodded to the driver. The driver gunned his engine to life, stifled a yawn. They cruised back the way they had come.

17

Claire wondered how she would stand it.

She had been tempted to take the day off from work, but had changed her mind and come to the office at the last minute. If she failed to show up there might be questions asked. Jack Rhodes would be in constant touch with the police, keeping them informed on the behaviour of the staff. A glimmer of suspicion aimed at her could quickly turn into a dazzling spotlight.

But she wished she had stayed away. There was Blake Denton at his desk behind her, and she couldn't rid herself of the sensation of Denton's bright eyes drilling accusingly between her shoulder blades. He knew what she knew, and what he didn't know he had managed to fill in with extremely accurate guess-work.

Of course Case had gone to murder Denton in his sleep last night and of course he had made a hash of it. On hearing from Denton something had curled up inside her and died. It was hope, likely. She had waited a while and then called Jim Case, asking him bluntly if he had been to Denton's apartment. At first he had hedged and blustered, but finally he had admitted it, telling her to forget the incident as it was none of her business.

How could she forget it? How could she forget the fact that Case was a heartless killer? Could she run away with a killer, live with him? And what about the police? She had the feeling they were watching her as well as Denton. A net had been flung wide, but was gradually being drawn in. She was scared. She was caught in a trap. If only there was some way she could break free of it and escape . . .

That morning seemed an eternity to Claire. No matter how hard she tried to concentrate on her work she found it impossible. With Denton sitting there behind her she squirmed restlessly, endeavouring to control her nervousness. He knew she was sweating and he was enjoying the taste of getting some of his own back. And in that mood it was more than probable he would ultimately go to the police.

By the lunch hour Claire was near to breaking point. Denton stood up and looked at her. There was no expression on his features except for that stare in his eyes. She couldn't bring herself to meet his gaze squarely. She turned her head to see Kirk Mason regarding them thoughtfully. She hurried on out of the office.

Usually she drove to a little restaurant on Market Street. It was where she had eaten lunch during the two years she had been with *Advance*. Today she couldn't think of food. Instead she continued driving to the river that curled through the south end of town. She stood for a time, watching the small craft riding the muddy waters. The waters of the river were deep and inviting. Shuddering, she turned away. Her attention was drawn to a man across the way who was leaning on the door of a car and watching her intently. Her breath caught in her throat. The man wasn't looking at her now, but she judged he was a police officer.

Panic seized Claire. They were watching her after all. They had more evidence against her than she had been willing to believe. Perhaps they knew about Case as well, knew that the pair of them had planned the robbery of Hank Otis' twenty thousand dollars.

She was late in getting back to the office, having made a wide detour of side streets in order to ascertain whether she was being followed. She had seen no one trailing her in a car, but it didn't mean police weren't trailing her.

The afternoon dragged on for ever. At five Claire hurried down to her car and drove home. Away from furtive stares and accusing eyes, she collapsed in a heap on the couch and gave herself up to sobbing brokenly.

Later she pulled herself together and made coffee. When she looked at her reflection in a mirror she was devastated by the way her appearance had altered. She saw lines that had never been there, dark hollows beneath her eyes. Her eyes were wide and haunted.

She just couldn't go on like this.

Another day of the torture she was undergoing and she would be mad.

She waited for the phone to ring, for Blake Denton to call, or Jim Case to call, or the police to call. By eight o'clock a solution was formulating in her mind. There was only one avenue out of the fix she was in. She would have to go to the police and confess. They could do what they liked with her, but at least she would have relief from the punishing pressures building up in her. And her sanity would be saved.

First off she would have to tell Case.

She dialled his number at eight-thirty. He said he had just been about to ring her. How had things gone for her today?'

'I can't stand it, Jim,' she blurted out passionately. 'I couldn't face one more day at that office, not with Blake Denton there . . . '

'I told you to forget about Denton,' Case said sharply. 'All right, so I goofed last night. But it won't happen again, Claire, I promise you. You don't have to worry about the guy. He can't touch you. He can't make a move one way or the

283

other. If he does, then he knows he'll catch it in the neck.'

'I'm going to tell them, Jim.'

'What! What the hell are you talking about, Claire? Tell who? Tell what?'

'The police. I'm sure they're on to me, Jim. I think they're having me watched.' Claire rushed on despite Case's attempts to interrupt her. 'As I said before, Jim, you have the money that you wanted. You're in the clear. I won't mention your name. I'll give them a false name and a false description to throw them off the scent. Go and get the money and leave Maxwell at once . . . '

'You're crazy!' Case screeched. 'You're out of your mind, Claire. Do you figure the cops are dumb? They won't make you talk in straight language! Look,' he continued with more restraint, 'do nothing immediately, sweetie. Do you hear me? Am I registering?'

Claire laughed shortly.

'Of course I hear you, Jim. I'm not as crazy as you take me for. But I will be before long unless — '

'Good,' he cried. 'Good! Hold on,

baby. Cool it down. We've got to discuss this first of all. After we do then you can put on any disc you want for the cops.'

Claire gnawed at her underlip. She had never heard Case in this tone. It worried her. He was treating her as if she was fresh out of kindergarten. But the least she could do was grant his request. Then a thought hit her.

'You can't come here, Jim. If the police suspect anything they could be watching the apartment block. I could go to your place — '

'No,' he said flatly. 'Quit worrying, Claire. I'll get in without the cops seeing me. You have a window leading on to the fire escape?'

'Yes, but — '

'Open it when I tinkle, doll. I won't be long. And stay away from the phone, get it?'

'All right, Jim. I'll do as you say. But remember one thing, Jim. My mind is made up.'

'Sure, sure! We'll see. We've got to talk, honey.'

He hung up.

Detective 3rd grade Rex Scott, parked in an anonymous black radio car in Tunley Avenue, lifted his mike and spoke into it.

'Car thirty-two to Headquarters . . .'

'Come in, Rex,' Ed Raven said a moment later.

'Case has just left his apartment, Sergeant. He's walking to the Olds at the curb. Must be going someplace. What do we do?'

'You follow him,' Raven said tersely. 'Don't let him out of your sight.'

'Check, Sarge. He's on the move. We'll get glued to him.'

'Mind you don't make it obvious, Rex. Keep in touch.'

The Olds went off like a rocket leaving its launching pad. Scott snapped at his driver and the black car pulsed down the avenue in pursuit. They threaded street after street, the Olds keeping up the steam as if the driver's life depended on his haste.

At Lexington and Firth intersection a truck rumbled from the far side of the road, right into the path of the police vehicle. Rex Scott cursed. His driver went for the brakes. They were travelling too fast and the car crashed broadside into a high rear wheel of the truck. There was a crunch of metal that ran to a miniature explosion. Passers-by froze in horror. The first one to reach the police car saw the driver slumped over the wheel, his neck twisted at an unnatural angle. The man beside the driver had been flung over into the back seat. His eyes stared in a glazed, stunned manner and blood poured down his face. His lips moved as though he were trying to tell something.

★ ★ ★

On reaching St Ann's Avenue, Jim Case halted the Olds some two hundred yards short of the Biltmore apartment block, not wanting to run the risk of being spotted by a police observer. He had fancied a car was following him earlier and had heard a dull thump as he raced past the nose of a truck. There could have been an accident but he wasn't sure, and it didn't matter to him one way or the other.

His immediate problem was to get up to Claire's apartment without being seen.

He left the street and negotiated a rough stretch of waste ground, and five minutes later he was on the shadowy paved back yard of the apartment building. He saw the fire escape staircase and moved towards it. All he had to do was count the floors and calculate accurately which apartment the girl lived in.

Three flights up he spotted a blob of light in the surrounding darkness. There were a lot of lights on but the shades made an effective shield against the light escaping. The blob must indicate the window of Claire's back room. She had had the presence of mind to make a marker for him to follow.

He reached the window at last, peered in. He saw Claire standing by the wall, her head tilted high, her eyes closed, as if she were in a trance or were praying.

Case knuckle-rapped the glass.

Claire hurried forward and opened the

window for him. Case threw a leg across the sill and stepped into the room. He grinned at Claire, noting how white she was, how strung up with tension.

'I told you I'd make it, sweetie.'

'Are you sure no one followed you, Jim? Where did you leave your car?'

'A good piece along the road,' he said. 'Quit worrying will you I'm much too smart for the crummy jerks masquerading as cops.'

He drew the blind down and took her through to the living room. She swung to face him, bosom heaving. He could see that her mind was made up and nothing he might say would alter her intentions.

'Now let's have it, Claire,' he said. 'You're jittery but you'll get over it. Hell, you'll just have to cope and get over it, won't you? Where is that old spirit you used to have, huh? Here, give me a kiss . . . '

She wouldn't let him kiss her. There was a look in her eyes that was akin to revulsion. Fear was there as well, fear of him. It triggered a mighty anger in his bloodstream.

'What *is* the matter with you, sweetie? You've never been like this. Don't tell me it's on account of the dumb punk, Denton? Say! You wouldn't have fallen for him?'

'No, I haven't,' she said bitterly. 'But you should have left him alone. You shouldn't have tried to kill him. You can't kill him, Jim. You can't go around killing everybody who stands in your way.'

'Let me decide that,' he said thinly. 'So you've gone soft like I hoped you wouldn't. You want to see the tail-end of old Jim. Is that it, baby. Is that it!'

'No, Jim, no . . . '

He was closing with her again and she backed away from him. She backed until she was against the wall and could go no further. Then real fear grabbed her by the throat. There was a shine in Case's eyes that sent wild panic beating in her veins.

She ducked under the arms that stretched out to her, ran to a dresser and stooped to pull open the bottom drawer. She snatched up the .32 automatic she had carried ever since Las Vegas. She had carried that gun with her for years, using it only once and that for harmless target practice. The clip was always loaded but she had no idea of the condition the shells were in.

Feverishly she pushed off the safety catch, spun to Jim Case.

His shoe crashed against her wrist and the automatic went spinning into a corner. They went after it like two dogs after a bone. Claire got to the gun first, grabbed it. Case's big hand clamped over her knuckles. They wrestled, Claire fighting as she had never fought in her life. She was fighting for her life. Case was intent on killing her.

The gun banged sharply.

On the same instant something slammed Claire to the floor. The bullet had hit her just under the right breast and blood was spewing furiously.

Case stood looking at her, his features gathered up in tortured disbelief. The automatic fell to the rug.

'No!' he panted. 'No Claire, I didn't mean to — '

Something snapped in him. He wheeled and headed for the back window, dragging the blind with such force it ripped clear of its moorings. The window open, he hurried on to reach the catwalk. He tripped and went to his knees, gathered himself up and went on to the iron staircase. His feet beat down the stairway in a mad tattoo.

★　★　★

Denton drove up to the Biltmore block and sat staring through the shadows. He had reached the end of his tether and saw only one way out of the dilemma. He would have to pressure Claire Paige to force her to talk. He was fed up to the teeth with being harried from pillar to post like a hunted animal. Last night's attempt on his life was the last straw. Claire had no feeling for him and he wasn't obliged to try and shield her. The tall stranger could try some more of his strong-arm stuff if the urge possessed him. This time he would be ready for the guy. He would give as much as he took and more if the opportunity afforded.

There was no sign of the Olds sitting

on the parking area, but Claire's car was there, and it meant she was at home. He could see no waiting patrol cars either and that was all to the good. He didn't care a lot if the police did close in on them now. He would tell everything he knew and had done and would fix it so that Claire would sing also.

Denton was leaving his car when he heard an engine grind to life along the road. As soon as the motor caught the vehicle surged off into darkness, hitting the unmade road as though it was a tank instead of an auto.

Frowning, he went into the lobby and took the elevator to the seventh floor. There was a queer nagging doubt at the back of his mind, and it gathered substance as he tramped the passage to reach Claire's door.

He rang the bell and waited. There was no answer. He gripped the door handle and pushed. The door was locked from the inside.

A muffled groan trickled out to his ears, a thin, despairing cry.

Denton delayed no further. Stepping

off to the wall of the passage he threw himself bodily at the door. There was a wrenching, cracking sound and the lock gave. The door burst inward. Denton hurried on to the living room, coming up short at sight of the redhead on the floor.

She wasn't dead but she was dying; Denton was convinced of this. Blood had made a wet rag of her dress. That and the small automatic lying nearby told him the story. The breeze blowing through from the open rear window provided its own confirmation to the theory building in his mind.

Claire's eyelids fluttered and he stooped over her, taking a white slender hand in his own.

'Claire, it's me . . . Blake . . . Can you hear me? Who did this?'

'Blake . . . It was Jim. He shot me . . . '

'Jim who, honey? Where does he hang out?'

Haltingly she told him. She spoke so faintly he had to bend closer to hear what she said.

'Tunley Avenue . . . One, one, five

. . . Apartment house. But, Blake . . . listen . . .'

'Later,' he said roughly, straightening and going to the phone. He dialled Police Headquarters and rapped curt instructions into the mouthpiece. He hung up on the questions that were flung at him. Swinging, he glanced at the automatic on the floor, reached down and lifted it. He stuffed it into his jacket pocket.

With a last look at the girl on the rug he sprang on out of the apartment, having to brush aside a knot of curious roomers who had come to see what the racket was about.

★　★　★

Around the time that Denton was calling Police Headquarters, Kirk Mason was entering the doorway diffidently. He was taken to the desk sergeant who scribbled down what he had to tell him.

The sergeant peered at him through shaggy brows.

'A five-dollar bill? Well, I don't know. But you could have something. Wait a minute and I'll see if Ed Raven is available.'

Mason said he would wait. He wondered if he had done the right thing in coming here. He hoped he wouldn't be responsible for landing Blake Denton in trouble.

18

Denton was slamming himself into the Volkswagen as a car drove up to the front of the apartment building and stalled. Two police officers piled out. It was a prowl car that had been close to the vicinity and directed to investigate the telephone message.

Denton drove on out of the street. He had a rough idea about the direction to Tunley Avenue, but he would find it all right and when he did he would take care of the character called Case. It was Case who had been Claire's confederate, and Case who had tried to murder him in his bed. He had already murdered Hank Otis and now he had done for his girl friend. Whatever the reasons for Claire getting together with such a partner, and whatever the reasons for his shooting her, he was a mad animal to be tracked down and destroyed.

Driving to Tunley Avenue, Denton

thought of the money. Did the guy called Case have the twenty grand and was that what the spat with Claire had been about? He wanted to cut adrift from her and keep the dough for himself?

More questions begging answers! He didn't have any solid answers to supply. At the moment he must play the tune by ear.

He reached Tunley Avenue in twenty minutes from leaving the Biltmore block. He was turning a corner to enter the avenue when a car surged out of it and swung off to Denton's left. A brief glimpse was enough to tell him it was the Oldsmobile with Jim Case at the wheel.

Denton made a sharp U-turn and went after him. Further down the street he heard police sirens coming to life. Headlamps lanced through the darkness and Denton tramped on the accelerator, wanting to overtake Case before the cops did.

It was evident they had been watching him and were trying to get to grips with him. Likely they had been keeping his apartment under surveillance and waiting for him to turn up. And Case, spotting the police vehicle in time, had not halted at all, but spun about and made a run for it.

In and out of side streets and back alleys they went, Case doing his utmost to shake the cops. He hardly knew that Denton, too, was following him, so that Denton had this small advantage.

Ten minutes later the police car was no longer behind Denton. It had taken a wrong turning or been forced to stop somewhere. Denton kept the rear lights of the Oldsmobile in view. They were cutting out from the suburbs. Beyond here was open country, and it meant Case was endeavouring to flee Maxwell for good.

Out on the highway there was a pretty thick flow of traffic and Denton gritted his teeth, wishing for a bigger engine beneath the hood. Slowly but surely the Olds was getting away from him. At a cross-roads he saw a car swing to the right, making for the wild back country. He couldn't be sure it was the car Case drove. And then it hit him. Of course. That was the direction you would take to reach Fosset's woods. So the car must belong to the killer and he must have taken Claire's tip to hide the twenty grand in the woods.

Exhilaration swept Denton. If only the guy knew it he was heading to a trap.

He slowed at the cross-roads, made the turning on to the narrow road that was little better than a dirt track. By now the Olds was out of sight but the dim glow of its headlamps cutting into the darkness gave a rough indication of his position. Denton took it easy. At this stage of the game he didn't wish to alert Case. He would like to take him by surprise, like to have the opportunity of telling him what he thought of him before he sent a bullet at him. There was no doubt in his mind that he was going to shoot Case. You didn't show mercy to a mad dog.

He dropped his speed to a crawl on the approach to the woods. By now he was driving with his lights dead so that Case would not be alarmed. As the killer was in a hurry, he would simply park, dash from his car and recover the money. Then he would keep going away from Maxwell.

Denton halted when he saw a dull shadow up ahead. It was the outline of the Oldsmobile sitting on the edge of a clearing. He switched off the engine and climbed out, taking the .32 from his pocket.

He stood still for a few minutes, giving his eyes time to grow accustomed to the gloom. A pinpoint of light through the trees and dense undergrowth guided him like a beacon.

Denton began walking towards it.

He had to move carefully as the earth was littered with dried leaves and brittle dead branches. At each step small twigs crackled underfoot. The flashlight carried by Case had been swinging from side to side, but now it had been lowered to the ground and Denton saw the big man silhouetted in the fine beam.

He was stooped and wielding a shovel. The sounds of the digging blotted out the faint noise Denton was making. A bare six yards separated them, five yards, four . . .

Now Denton could see the killer clearly. He hadn't buried the briefcase deeply. He threw the shovel aside and bent to lift it.

'All right, Case, I've got you covered. Don't move.'

If he expected Case to obey him he was disappointed. With a savage curse he snatched a gun from his pocket and began firing. He went into action so fast he took Denton by surprise. Bullets whistled and whined amongst the trees; one snapped off a thin branch directly above Denton's head.

Denton triggered twice and Jim Case screamed. He sagged in two like a loosely-packed sack of grain, all the while moaning and cursing, his breath tearing in his throat.

Just then Denton heard sirens yammering along the dirt road. The police were coming. Somehow or other they had picked up the trail, or learned where Case had hidden the stolen money.

Denton stood where he was, listening to the hoarse breathing of the killer. He was down on the ground, grovelling with his hands. Finally he stopped grovelling and was still.

Denton didn't move from the spot. He was there when the police swarmed through the trees, strong flashlights sweeping the terrain. They soon saw him.

'Drop that gun, buddy! Drop it like I say . . .'

Denton dropped the gun. Three big cops closed with him and frisked him. Then they bundled him out of the woods to the cars. They pushed him into the back seat of one of the cars.

Doors slammed. The car went into rocking motion, surging for the highway that would take them on to Maxwell.

★   ★   ★

He was seated in Lieutenant Granger's office, listening to the lieutenant talk. He could scarcely believe what was being said.

'The dame didn't die at once, Denton,' Granger said bleakly. 'She was able to tell us a story. She told how she tricked you into going to the warehouse that night. She sent you there to collect some important documents she had left behind

303

and that she wanted to do some home-work on. Her pal was waiting for you. Only, her pal wasn't waiting for Hank Otis to turn up, and that's what happened. This guy Case shot Otis, then slugged you. You got out over the roofs. That was her story, Denton,' Granger went on thinly. 'She didn't explain the duplicate key we found, the shovel we found, the gloves we found. But she did let you out, pal, so you've got something to be grateful to her for. Afterwards you suspected she had pulled a gag on you. You figured you were so tough and brainy you could sort it out for yourself. You didn't reckon on Case shooting the dame as well.'

'I — '

'Shut up Denton. My patience with you is wearing mighty slender. You could have balled things up for us. You did ball things up for us. Why the hell didn't you come and tell us all about it in the first place? We have had two officers killed.'

'But Claire — '

'Yeah, Claire,' Granger interrupted him again. 'You thought you knew everything about her. You didn't know anything, buster. She used to be a club hostess in Las Vegas. She lived there with this guy Case. She — Aw, what's the use. You're dumb and you'll always be dumb. But you knocked over Case and that's something to your credit. We could have you for breaking and entering, I guess. But what the hell. A dumb cluck is a dumb cluck in any man's language. Get out of here, Denton. But be back here first thing in the morning to make a formal statement. Get it, buster?'

'Sure,' Denton mumbled. 'Sure. But — '

'Like I say,' Granger scowled. 'Take off, will you. Until morning, bright boy. Think it over. Sleep on it. Now beat it if you don't want to spend the night in a cell.'

'Sure,' Denton said hoarsely. 'I understand.'

He left the office and walked drunkenly to the street. On the street he paused to drag fresh air to his lungs. His mind was buzzing. He couldn't even think straight. But yes, he could. He knew what he had to do right now — head for the nearest phone booth and ask Olive Overton if she was too busy to listen to a long story.

We do hope that you have enjoyed reading this large print book.

Did you know that all of our titles are available for purchase?

We publish a wide range of high quality large print books including:
Romances, Mysteries, Classics
General Fiction
Non Fiction and Westerns

Special interest titles available in large print are:
The Little Oxford Dictionary
Music Book, Song Book
Hymn Book, Service Book

Also available from us courtesy of Oxford University Press:
Young Readers' Dictionary
(large print edition)
Young Readers' Thesaurus
(large print edition)

For further information or a free brochure, please contact us at:
Ulverscroft Large Print Books Ltd.,
The Green, Bradgate Road, Anstey,
Leicester, LE7 7FU, England.
Tel: (00 44) 0116 236 4325
Fax: (00 44) 0116 234 0205